Praise for *Small!*

'A GIANT triumph! Funny, creative & heart-warming,
I adored everything from the hilarious giant-school
timetables to the swamp fish & bogweed sandwiches.
And who wouldn't want a best friend like Walloping
Toenail? Loved this MG!'

A.F. Steadman, author of
Skandar and the Unicorn Thief

'A funny, heartwarming delightful début'

The Bookseller, One to Watch

'Small! Is vast in humour and heart. A giant of a book'
Zillah Bethell, author of *The Shark Caller*

'With enormous guffaws, unspeakable peril and a
giant heart, I'm sure SMALL will be a MAHOOSIVE
hit!'
Bethany Walker, author of

l Me

'Richly imagined and packed with humour and heart'
Booklover Jo, author of
Libby and the Parisian Puzzle

'Small is big on fun, huge on heart and full of guffaws.
The story of Harvey Small's friendship with Walloping
the giant is enough to warm a swamp goblin's heart.'
Myles McLeod, author of the
Knight Sir Louis series

'It's funny, it's silly and it's simply delightful! Fun
with a giant-sized 'F'!'
Rashmi Sirdeshpande, author of
Never Show a T-Rex a Book

'It's epic. Massive fun, giant amounts of silliness and a
huge heart. I loved every page of it.'
Tom Vaughan, author of Bin Boy

'A totally original tall tale that's spurt-your-tea-out
funny.'
Lucy Brandt, author of,
Leonora Bolt: Secret Inventor

About the author

Hannah Moffatt is a creative director at a language and behavioural science consultancy, where she spends her days writing very sensible things for businesses. At night, she escapes into the beautifully bonkers world of middle grade fiction, where she writes significantly less sensible things for children. Hannah lives in London with her husband and a sombrero-wearing toy hedgehog named Cedric.

Small!

Hannah Moffatt

Published in the UK by Everything with Words Limited
Fifth Floor, 30–31 Furnival Street, London EC4A 1JQ

www.everythingwithwords.com

Text copyright © Hannah Moffatt 2022
Cover © Holly Ovenden 2022
Illustrations © Rory Walker 2022

Printed and bound in Great Britain by
CPI Group (UK) Ltd, Croydon CRO 4YY

A CIP catalogue record for this book is available from the British Library.

ISBN 978-1-911427-27-8

For Mum and Dad – my bricks

Beware! Swamp Goblins!

My name is Harvey Small. You can call me a human. But not a bogeyman or a goblin or a vampire … and certainly not a giant.

Mum's job makes us move a lot. I've lived in Small Town, Small City, Small-on-the-Hill, Small-over-the-Hill, Small-round-the-Hill, Small-under-the-Hill, Smallshire, Smallford, Smallington and Small-on-Sea. And I've only ever seen humans there.

But I've got a secret.

If you drive night and day, and day and night and night and day again, you'll come to a deep, dark, stinky swamp. You won't see a single office block or any shops or cinemas or football grounds … only thick green weeds, boggy ground and faded signs that say, '*Beware! Swamp Goblins!*'

And all those creatures you thought lived in stories? You'll find them there. Some of them, anyway.

The world is far bigger than grown-ups say.

I know.

I've seen it.

Chapter one

Bang!

O n my 10th birthday, I opened:

- one pair of stilts
- one pair of sludge-brown dungarees that were ten times too long for me
- one green velvet top hat that was almost half a metre high and fell over my nose
- absolutely NO football boots.

"Thanks Mum," I said, struggling to hide my disappointment. Mum's presents were even worse than that shower cap Aunty Hilda gave me last year.

"Go on, try them on," said Mum. She picked up

the stilts and put them on the kitchen floor. She had an eager look in her eyes.

I shook my head. I didn't feel like fancy dress.

"Come on, spoil sport. Look, you stand on these flat bits here," said Mum. She pointed at two shoe-sized platforms halfway up each stilt. They had straps dangling off them. "I'll strap in your trainers. Then you can walk around and pretend to be really tall. You'll love it." Mum beamed at me like this was a brilliant idea.

It wasn't.

I'm Harvey Small, not Harvey Tall. Being short didn't bother me. Short kids could still play football. If they had new football boots. Which I didn't.

Mum lifted me onto the stilts anyway, and my head almost hit the ceiling.

I looked down and frowned.

Each stilt had a flipper-sized

4

fake foot sticking out the bottom. "What are the feet for?" I asked. This was definitely the weirdest present I'd ever had.

"Oh," said Mum, laughing a little too loudly. "I think rubber feet make stilts *even more fun*, don't you? Go on, try walking around."

Mum's idea of fun wasn't the same as mine.

I took one step forwards, went "Woaahhhhhh!" and fell flat on the kitchen floor.

"Ow!" I said.

"Oops," said Mum, unstrapping me from the stilts. She looked at her watch and frowned like she was late for something. But we couldn't be late. Mum promised she wouldn't go to work on my birthday. And I didn't have school because Mum hadn't found a new one for me yet.

Not after what happened in the last one.

Or the one before that.

Was that why Mum got me such awful presents? I was still trying to work it out, when there was a knock on the door.

BANG.

It wasn't a normal knock.

BANG!

5

Sawdust came down from the ceiling.

BANG!

The whole house shook.

"That must be the new neighbours, coming to wish you a happy birthday!" said Mum in the pretend cheery voice she uses when she doesn't want me to worry. (It *always* makes me worry more.)

"But no one lives anywhere near here!" I blurted as all our plates fell off the kitchen shelf and smashed on the floor. Unlike our boring old houses on boring streets next to boring offices, *this* house was on the edge of a swamp. It smelled like damp raincoats and looked ready to fall down. I loved it.

"Let's surprise them!" said Mum, acting like I hadn't said anything at all. She shoved the top hat on my head, lifted me back onto the stilts and pulled the extra-long dungarees up over them.

"Mum, what are you doing?" I said. If our new neighbours really were outside, this wasn't what I wanted to wear when I met them.

Mum ignored me again and pushed me into the hall. I wobbled all the way.

BANG!

BANG!

CRASH!

A big hairy fist burst through the middle of the front door and pulled it off its hinges.

"Arghhhhhhhhhhhhhhhhhhhhhhhhhhhhh!" I cried.

The hairy fist was attached to a hairy arm that was attached to a body that was even bigger than mine (and I was on STILTS!). This body was so tall its face could have peered into our upstairs windows. But right now, the face and the arms and the fists and the body were bent over and squeezing through the space where our front door had been.

There was only one sensible thing to do.

"HELP! IT'S A GIANT! HE'S GOING TO EAT US!" I yelled at the top of my voice. I stumbled backwards so fast I almost fell off my stilts.

But the strangest thing of all was Mum. She didn't scream, or cry, or call the police. She said, "Oh, you must be Mr Ogg. Thank you *so* much for coming."

Then she pointed at me.

"This is my son, Harvey. I think he'll fit in perfectly at your school."

School? What kind of school would want stilt-walking students? Or have giants for teachers?

"I'm sure Madame Bogbrush's School for Gifted Giants will be the *perfect* place for my gifted boy," Mum added.

So that's what she was up to.

Nice try, Mum. But even when I was wobbling on stilts, there was NO WAY Mr Ogg would think I was a giant.

Not a chance.

Uh uh.

Absolutely not.

Chapter two

A Giant-sized Test

So, there I was, wobbling all over the place on my new stilts. And Mr Ogg, the giant who'd smashed into our house, was squeezing himself into the kitchen. He had all the grace of a rhino climbing through a cat flap.

I stared, open-mouthed at the giant.

The giant stared back at me.

At any second, I expected him to point out the obvious fact that I, Harvey Small, was not a giant. I waited for him to tell Mum that I couldn't possibly go to Madame Bogbrush's School for Gifted Giants. I hoped he'd clomp away again, without bashing us with his huge, hairy fists.

Mr Ogg stamped his feet.

Mum and I jumped a metre off the floor.

"**You not giant**," said Mr Ogg. The force of his breath blew me into the fridge door.

I knew it. I knew we couldn't fool a giant.

Except Mr Ogg wasn't talking to me. He was prodding a jumbo-sausage-roll-sized finger into Mum's chest.

This was terrible.

Mum was so desperate to find a school for me, she'd invited a giant teacher to tea. Now he was definitely going to bash her! And it was all my fault! I had to do something.

"**Giants don't like Smalls**," said the giant. "**Giants *stomp* on Smalls**." He stamped his foot again, smashing through a floorboard.

Smalls? How could ALL giants not like Mum and me? Mr Ogg had only just met us!

I stood, frozen on the spot. A bead of sweat dripped down Mum's forehead. But she didn't give up.

"Smalls? Yuck! We can't stand them either!" she said. "I'm not a Small. I'm a Country Giant. I'm an extremely rare short breed. You can tell I'm a giant because I've got a giant son. And ... he's the brightest in his year!"

Ohhh. When Mr Ogg said he didn't like Smalls, he meant he didn't like *humans.* I wasn't sure that made things better.

Mr Ogg narrowed his big brown eyes and peered at me again.

"My boy's so hard-working," said Mum.

"Ogg be judge of that," said Mr Ogg. When he spoke, his hot breath hit me like a blast of Mum's hairdryer. It smelled like boiled eggs.

My stomach churned.

"What be one plus one?" asked the giant, staring straight at me.

I didn't want to mess with him. And I didn't want Mum to get bashed. But I couldn't go to giant school, either. So, I did the only sensible thing. "One plus one is one hundred and eight," I said. Mum glared at me.

"Hmm," said Mr Ogg, scratching the three tufts of black hair that stuck out from his otherwise bald head. **"Yes, one hundred and eight. Sounds right. Boy know numbers,"** said the giant, giving me a hot, eggy smile.

So much for being a school for *gifted* giants, I thought.

"Haha. Yes, that's my little, um, mathematician," said Mum. She shot me a stern, I'm-the-grown-up-and-I-know-best-so-don't-you-dare-say-a-word look.

"When can he start school?"

"**Not yet**," said Mr Ogg, shaking his head. "**Giant must be strong. Show me strong.**" Mr Ogg flexed his own muscles, sending his clenched fists through the ceiling.

There was NO WAY I'd pass this test. Compared to a giant I wasn't

strong at all. Even compared to kids my own age, I was on the weedy side.

But Mum edged over and gave me a sneaky push.

That's all it took.

I lurched forwards, plunging my right stilt leg through the middle of a kitchen chair.

CRASH!

I swiped a vase of flowers with my flailing arms.

SMASH!

I tumbled head-first into the opposite wall.

SMACK!

And the one shelf that hadn't fallen off when Mr Ogg bashed his way in, clattered onto the kitchen floor.

I rubbed my bumped head (top hats make rubbish crash helmets) and gawped at the mess. Mum fluttered her eyelashes at Mr Ogg. "See how strong he is?" she said. "He's completely ruining my lovely new home."

"**Boy be strong. Good. One more test,**" said Mr Ogg, still staring at me.

This time, I couldn't stare back. My head throbbed. My stomach gurgled. I felt dreadful.

"**Madame Bogbrush love music. Sing me song,**" ordered Mr Ogg.

Even if I'd wanted to sing (which I didn't) it would have been completely impossible. My head spun so much that...

BLURRRRGHHHHHHHH!

I puked all over the floor.

Mr Ogg clapped his hands, sending the last of our chairs flying.

He gave me a wide grin, flashing three wonky rotten teeth. "**Boy has voice of angel**," he said, spitting into his wide hand and holding it out to me. I looked at the green blobs of drool dripping from the giant's fingers.

I thought I was going to be sick all over again.

"Go on," said Mum, nudging me. "Shake Mr Ogg's hand." It seemed completely crackers, but Mum clearly wanted me to get a place in giant school. I couldn't disappoint her. Not again.

I closed my eyes and tried not to squeal as Mr Ogg's slimy hand clenched mine.

"**Boy goes to our school,**" said Mr Ogg.

Then, just like that, the giant turned and *CLOMP*, *CLOMP*, *CLOMPED* out of our house.

And Mum had some giant-sized explaining to do.

Chapter three

The Rules

I blinked at the crumbling remains of our kitchen. Had I really just got a place in a school for *giants?*

"Well done, Harve, my *gifted* little giant!" said Mum. She unstrapped my stilts and pulled me into a hug. "Oh, I'm going to miss you!"

"Miss me? What do you mean, *miss me?*" I asked.

Mum bit her lip.

"Listen, I know you don't like changing schools every time I install *doo dahs* and network *thingy-mabobs* for new companies. Now you won't have to." (That might not be *exactly* what Mum said. I don't always listen properly when she talks about work.)

"Madame Bogbrush says most gifted giants stay

in school," said Mum. "Isn't that lucky? You can live there and make lots of lovely gifted giant friends."

Friends.

Mum was right about one thing. I did want to make *proper* friends. Mum had worked extra hard since Dad left, and we'd moved loads to be closer to all her offices. It would be nice to stay in one place for a while.

Maybe giant school wouldn't be so bad.

Except...

"But I'll get squashed!" I cried. "Mr Ogg said he stomps on Smalls!"

"*Only* if he finds out you're not a giant. Stay on your stilts and he probably won't stomp on you ... or pound you into a pancake ... or flatten you into a sandwich. I'm almost certain," said Mum.

"A SANDWICH?!" I cried. How could Mum look so calm?

"Don't be such a worry wart, Harvey. Honestly, you'd think I was sending you to the Unspeakable Circus!"

I shuddered. We've all heard the stories. About the kids who mysteriously disappear. Everyone knows they end up in the Unspeakable Circus. I bet most of them get eaten by zombie clowns. If this was Mum's way of making me feel better, it wasn't working.

"Hang on," she said, leaving the room. A second later, Mum stumbled back in carrying a ginormous green book. It said 'THE RULES' on the cover.

Mum dropped the book on the kitchen table.

The table broke in half.

"Madame Bogbrush sent you these. Follow the school rules and you'll be *fine*," she said. "Break them, and there's the teensiest chance she'll stomp you into a sandwich. But you're such a good boy, I know there's nothing to worry about."

I gawped at the rule book. It looked about a million pages long. Mum was wrong. I had *everything* to worry about.

"Does Dad know about this?" I asked. He moved out two years ago. But surely he wouldn't want his only son to be squashed by giants.

"It was his idea," said Mum.

Oh.

Of course.

It all made sense. Or, I should say, it all made sense to *me*. If you're reading my story, it probably won't make sense to you. That's because there's something you don't know about me yet. I'm *bad* news. Seriously. When I'm around, bad things always happen, even though I don't mean them to. Like the time I forgot to wear my lucky socks to watch Smallington Rovers (my favourite football team) play at home. They lost five-nil. Or the time Olivia Little was in the school play and I said, 'break a leg' (because I'd heard that's how you wish actors luck). Then she slipped on the stage steps and *actually broke her leg*. She went around telling everyone I'd cursed her.

But by far the worst thing I've ever done is to Mum and Dad.

It is my fault they split up.

It was my old football boot Dad tripped over the night they had the BIG FIGHT. Dad never mentioned it, but I know he still blamed me.

"Don't give me that face. I'm sure you *won't* become a sandwich," said Mum.

I shook my head.

"I'm sorry, but with your," Mum paused. "...
record, it's getting hard to find a normal school that'll take you. They're either full or they've heard what happened to Rodney Hamster..."

Poor Rodney. When I was in Small Lane Primary, I took Rodney Hamster home for the weekend, and he DIED. Miss Tiny said it wasn't my fault. Rodney was almost four years old (which is about a hundred in hamster years). But I looked it up afterwards and I definitely wasn't supposed to feed him spaghetti bolognese, even though it's yummy. The whole school called me Harvey Hamster Killer after that.

"Then there was that incident with the trifle," said Mum. I blushed just thinking about it. "And setting fire to the Headteacher's trousers..." she added. See? I'm bad news.

"But giants aren't interested in Small school reports. So, there's no problem. That's why we moved next to the swamp. Madame Bogbrush only takes local giants."

"I'm not a giant!"

"It was either this or Master Ghoulish's Academy for Failing Bogeymen. And my son's no failure."

"Bogeymen?!" I cried. All this time I thought the world was just full of humans like me. Now Mum was saying bogeymen were as real as giants! My brain exploded like a mouthful of popping candy.

"I'll visit when I can," said Mum. "But I have to go back to Small City for a while. For work. And your school is *very* far away from all the Small towns."

She was right about that. To get here, we'd driven through the town, the village, the countryside, the woodland, the marshes, the bogland, no man's land, the Plains of Despair and the Point of No Return.

Finally, we arrived on the edge of the Stinking, Sinking Swamp. It took days.

"So that's it? You're leaving me?" I said.

"Don't be silly," said Mum, putting her hand on my shoulder. "We've got *a whole week* to turn you into a giant."

It was official. Mum had lost it. I might have fooled Mr Ogg, but there was absolutely no way I'd fool an entire school of gifted giants by Monday. It was totally and utterly impossible.

The Rules (*continued*)   13

You will be stomped into a sandwich if:

28.   You're a Small
29.   You pick your toenails during dinner
30.   You sneak in the corridors
31.   You get algae on your best grunting dungarees
32.   You leave your dorm room at night FOR ANY REASON
33.   You don't eat your bogweed
34.   You stomp things in pounding class
35.   You pound things in stomping class
36.   You're friends with a Small

Chapter four

Into the Swamp

The next week went by in a stilt-stumbling daze.
I tripped.

I hit my head.

I grazed my knees.

Most of my skin turned plum-crumble purple from my 67 new bumps and bruises. (I counted them all.)

But I'd finally worked out the secret to walking on stilts.

Marching.

If you keep your back straight, your tummy tight, and march your feet like the guards outside Smallington Palace, you won't fall over.

I'd just gone a whole day without crashing into

anything. And, you know what? I made a pretty convincing giant.

Now, Mum and I stood in the front garden. I'd packed my things. Even Lord Pawington Bear-Face Grumple Snout the Second. Or Mr Snout (my secret favourite teddy) for short. Mum and Dad bought him for me when I was five. That was years before the BIG FIGHT. His right eye was loose and his fur was faded, but Mr Snout was my best friend. I didn't care that rule 178 in Madame Bogbrush's book said, 'No teddy bears.' I'd stashed him between my clean underpants and spare top hats. No one would look there.

"Mr Ogg said he'll collect you himself, isn't he a sweetie?" said Mum.

She must have gone stark raving bananas if she thought that hairy-fisted, door-punching giant was a *sweetie*. I couldn't think of anything WORSE than being escorted to school by a *teacher*.

Mum could. She shuffled me towards the gate.

"I've got to get back to work in Small City. Kipper socks are at an all-time low. If we buy now, we'll get big profiteroles." (At least I *think* that's what she said. Mum's job is weird. But I like profiteroles. They're my favourite pudding.)

"I need to get through the Point of No Return before sunset. You'll be okay here, won't you, Harve?" said Mum.

"Hang on, so you're not waiting for Mr Ogg?" I said.

Mum looked at me and smiled. "My little boy, all grown up."

"I'm NOT grown up. I'm ON STILTS!" I said. Mum hopped into the car.

I panicked. "You can't leave me. What if Mr Ogg doesn't come?"

"Oh, giants are never late," said Mum, starting the car. "Their watches are huge."

"No! Mum, wait!" I cried.

"Don't forget to write!" she said. "You can't call. The swamp has terrible phone reception!" Mum waved out the window. "I love you Harvey-Poo. Remember, stay on your stilts and you'll be fine." Then she sped off, over the hill and away.

I gave a wobbly wave. I felt so … alone.

The feeling didn't last long.

A minute later, I heard the *brum* of a car engine and sighed with relief. Mum must be coming back.

Except the car didn't belong to Mum.

24

It wasn't even a car.

It was a sludge-brown camper van, with monster truck tyres. And it was surrounded in a haze of billowing green smoke that smelled like sprouts. Hunched in the driver's seat, with his knees up to his shoulders, his elbows sticking out the windows and his head bursting through the sunroof, was Mr Ogg. I wondered why giants didn't have cars their own size.

Mr Ogg yelled out the sunroof. **"Get stuff. Get in."**

I hesitated.

Then I thought about the new friends Mum promised I'd make.

I picked up my suitcase and wobbled into the camper van.

"HOLD YER NOSE, BOY!" boomed Mr Ogg.

The van lurched forwards.

We burst through the barbed wire fence surrounding the Stinking, Sinking Swamp. We knocked down a sign saying, *'Beware! Swamp Goblins!'* and mud and sludge splattered the windows. I'd been dying to explore the swamp ever since I moved here. Now it whizzed by in a blur of green and brown. All the while a stench of cowpats and cabbage and old babies' nappies zoomed up my nose. I felt sick. Again.

My stomach gurgled.

"No singing in camper van!" said Mr Ogg. I nodded. I hoped I wouldn't do too much "singing" at school. Being sick wasn't fun.

"**Don't worry**," said Mr Ogg a moment later. "**Ogg know safe paths. No sinking in swamp for us!**"

I didn't just hold my breath. I gripped it for dear life.

As we drove deeper into the swamp, Mr Ogg slowed down.

"**Ogg careful. Paths narrow.**"

The trees grew thicker and the swamp grew darker.

My heart thudded against my seatbelt. It felt like the gloom was swallowing us.

Then there was the hissing.

Angry hissing.

Could a giant swamp have giant snakes in it?

I pushed my face against the glass, trying to see what was out there.

There was nothing…

Nothing…

Nothing…

Splat!

"Eeek!" I squealed, leaping back.

A cat-sized creature with pointy ears, a scrunched face and glowing yellow eyes, flew at us from the darkness. It stuck its rubbery paws to the camper van window.

"*Ssssss … stay away!*" it hissed.

My stilts and knees knocked together.

Mr Ogg tooted his horn and the creature scuttled into the dark.

"Don't mind Doris," said Mr Ogg. **"Swamp goblin can't eat you in van."**

I gave a shaky nod. I didn't want to ask where a swamp goblin *could* eat me.

We kept driving.

Eventually, the thick brown weeds and droopy green trees cleared.

The smell of boiling football socks died down.

I could see the sky again.

I was alive!

The camper van screeched to a halt in front of a pair of ornate golden gates, twisting into the clouds. Mr Ogg *creaaaaaked* them open.

"This be Madame Bogbrush's School for Gifted Giants," he said. **"Boy be home."**

The word "home" made my stomach flip. I stumbled out of the van and marched on the spot to stop myself wobbling.

A wonky green castle loomed on the horizon. In front of it stretched a muddy field as big as five football pitches. I hoped my new class played football.

A giant in sludge-brown dungarees like mine stumbled and squelched through the wet grass towards me. Would he believe I was a giant, too?

"Oh boy, oh boy, oh boy, a new classmate! We never gets new classmates!" said the squelching giant. "I is Walloping Toenail. Pleased to meets you," he said, pulling off his top hat and grinning at me.

Up close, Walloping was almost exactly as tall as me (on stilts). That was a good start.

He had greasy brown hair that stuck to his head. He had a dribbly, lopsided grin. And his hands were bigger than boxing gloves. Walloping Toenail did *not* look like the "nice gifted giant friends" Mum had in mind for me. He looked like he could eat me for breakfast.

"Where does you live?" he asked. "Ma says all the giants be here. I knew that be wrong. I wants to see the world. Can I come to your house?"

Before I could answer, three rusty green bells in three wonky green bell towers all clanged at once.

DING!

DANG!

DUNG!

I clamped my hands over my ears. The noise was so loud, the grass shook. Leaves fell from the trees. And a yellow-feathered bird that circled above us pooed on my shoes and *squawked* away.

"Oh boy, you is so lucky!" said Walloping, peering after the bird.

That's exactly the sort of thing Mum would say. But I for one didn't believe turning up to class with poo on my shoes was lucky.

"You only gets hit by a baby Swamp Flapper," added Walloping. "His Mum's bigger than me. If she splats you, you gets *flattened*. Happened to my Pa once. Took seven giants to dig him out!"

I wiped my shoes in the long grass. I'd keep a close eye on the sky from now on.

Walloping charged back across the field. "Hurry! I

can't wait for you to meets the class. They is going to be as excited as me to sees you!" He said, flinging a timetable at me.

A warm glow oozed through me like sticky toffee pudding. I don't think anyone had ever been excited to meet me when I started my old schools. Maybe I'd be happy here after all.

Timetable				
Monday	Tuesday	Wednesday	Thursday	Friday
Bashing things with clubs	Clobbering	Bashing things with bigger clubs	Double stomping	Advanced clomping
Group grunting	Pounding things with fists	Swamp survival training	Double stomping	Singing
Baking	Roaring: level 1	Maths	Performance grunting	Swamp gardening: mould care
Stomping things with feet	Grunting: theory	Arts and crafts (making clubs)	Bashing things with clubs: theory	Combined clobbering and clouting: level 3
Dinner	Dinner	Dinner	Dinner	Dinner

With my ears still ringing from the school bells, I wobbled after Walloping.

"It be Bashing Things with Clubs next! It's my bestest lesson!"

"Brilliant!"

That sounded loads more fun than science or geography or history ... or any lesson really. "What are we bashing?"

Walloping grinned. "Smalls, of course!"

I gulped.

Being a Small in giant school *might* be harder than I thought.

Chapter five

Do You Need the Toilet?

Smalls.

My class were bashing *Smalls!*

This was a total disaster. I was supposed to be making friends. But if just one beady-eyed giant spotted my stilts, they'd know *I* was a Small. I'd be bashed to bits in my very first lesson. If the school bells didn't blow my ears off first. They rang again, *even* louder and faster than before.

DINGDINGDING!
DANGDANGDANG!
DUNGDUNGDUNG!

Walloping Toenail, my dribbling giant guide, hurried us towards a crumbling, moss-covered castle.

I say 'castle,' it was more like a mountain with a front door. I've never seen anything so huge. Burning torches flickered up the walls. The whole place smelled like fire and felt like slime.

I hoped I'd live long enough to explore it.

My stomach bubbled with nerves as we stepped inside.

The **CLOMP** and **STOMP** of Walloping's massive feet echoed down the loooooooong, cold corridor.

"Here we is!" said Walloping, flinging a wooden

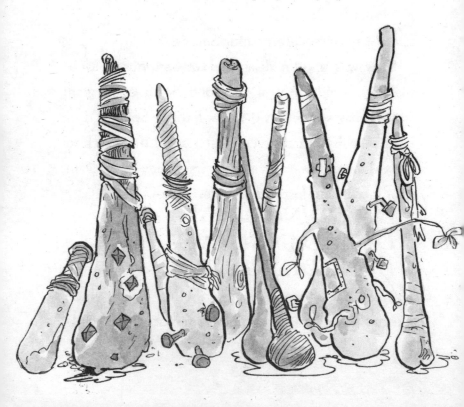

door open on a room that was about as big as my last school's whole assembly hall. I couldn't reach the ceiling, even if I was wearing ten pairs of stilts.

My heart pounded louder than the school bells.

This was it.

My moment to act like a giant, make friends … and NOT get bashed.

I followed Walloping in, keeping my best be-my-friend-I'm-not-bad-news-honest smile fixed to my face.

Not a single giant looked at me.

The class were busy fighting over a huge rack of chunky wooden clubs. It filled the back wall.

"I wants *Brain Squasher*. It's the best club and *I'm* the best basher."

"Fine, but it's my turn on *Toe Squelcher*!"

"Where's *Bum Basher* gone? Someone always steals my *Bum Basher!*"

Walloping pointed at me. "Look! Look! Look!" he said. "This be Harvey, our new classmate!"

Here's a tip. When you're meeting a class full of giants for the first time, try and do it when they're *not* carrying bashing clubs.

Ten sets of big gawking eyes bore into me. Thanks

to my stilts, the giants were about my size. But boy did they *feel* bigger.

My smile wobbled.

A boy with broad shoulders and clenched fists **Stomp, STOMP, STOMPED** across the stone floor towards me. He looked like he could flatten me in a second.

I *should* have held out my hand and said "Hello, I'm Harvey."

I *should* have tried to make friends.

Instead, I said "Eeeeeeeek!" and staggered back into the doorway.

Then, I said "Oooooof!"

No, the boy hadn't bashed me. I'd bumped straight into the biggest, scariest giant in the whole class. The one giant who was as big as Mr Ogg (who's almost as big as a house, remember). The giant in...

... THE FLOWERY DRESS AND ROUND PURPLE SPECTACLES!

Okay, maybe she wasn't *that* scary, but she *was* the teacher. And we all know what teachers are like.

"I see someone's got the first day jitters," she said.

Her breath smelled strangely of toasted marshmallows.
"I'm Mrs Mahoosive. You must be Harvey Small."

I think she was *trying* to be nice. But when the class heard my name, they roared with laughter. "Small?! Like the Smalls! **Hahahaha**!" they howled.

I marched on the spot to steady myself. Back in Small City, 'Small' was such a normal name. Here, it was hilarious. I felt my cheeks get hotter.

"Let's bash him!" said a girl with pigtails and gappy teeth.

The class raised their clubs.

And I did what any sensible kid would do.

I leaped behind the teacher.

The giants guffawed so much, tears fell from their eyes like waterfalls.

"Jumbolina, be nice!" said Mrs Mahoosive.

But when the class finished laughing, they went back to gawking. And that was *even* worse.

The boy with broad shoulders spoke up.

"Mrs Mahoosive, why are New Giant's hands so small?"

A giant girl with red hair piled up in a bun joined in. "Gallumphing Doorknob's right, Miss. Look at his arms. They're too short."

"**Norma Enormous!**" said the teacher, shaking her head.

I put my arms behind my back. It wasn't my fault. You couldn't get stilts for arms.

Just keep marching I told myself. Surely the only thing that could make this lesson worse was falling over.

Finally, a giant with watery eyes and a drippy nose waved his club at my legs.

"Miss, Miss, I think he needs a wee. He can't stand still!"

"**Lumbering Turnip, *that's enough!***" said the teacher. The blast of her angry breath made me wobble even more. Mrs

Mahoosive turned to me. "*Do you need the toilet?*"
she asked.

How humiliating.

"No!" I said. I'd had plenty of bad first days. But
this was one of the worst.

Mrs Mahoosive handed me a ginormous bashing
club. It was as long as my leg and as heavy as a grown-
up's bowling ball. I gripped it with all my might.
Maybe, just maybe, if I was brilliant at bashing,
everyone would stop talking about the toilet.

I took a deep breath and waved my club over my
head.

For one wonderful second, I held the club high.

This was it! I was doing it! I was just like a real
giant!

One second later, my arms turned to jelly. I
wobbled backwards, smashing my club into the
bookshelf behind me.

Two seconds later, I was buried up to my head
in a tumbling pile of textbooks. They had titles like,
Bashing for Beginners, *Clout Craft* and *Thwack Your
Way to the Top*.

"**Impressive bashing,**" said Mrs Mahoosive, blowing
dust off the books and placing them back on the shelf.

Norma Enormous, the giant with her hair in a bun, thudded over to help. She shot me a grumpy glare.

"**But today we're bashing *Smalls*, not *walls*,**" said the teacher.

How could I forget?

"**Gifted giants, there are four important things to know about Smalls,**" said Mrs Mahoosive, turning back to the class. They stood in a circle around her, beating their clubs menacingly against their chunky palms.

I gulped, wondering what Mrs Mahoosive was going to say.

"**One. Smalls don't like us,**" she said. Which wasn't true – I for one barely knew the giants.

"**Two. They're sneaky.**" I looked down at my giant costume. I guess Smalls are pretty sneaky.

"**Three. They do *unspeakable* things.**" I nodded again. Poor Rodney Hamster.

"**And four, worst of all, Smalls pick their nose...**" she gave a dramatic pause. "**...and eat it!**"

"Urghhhhh!" said the class, waving their clubs, stomping their feet and sticking their tongues out.

No. I didn't think that one was fair. I'd only picked my nose and eaten it once. Twice at most.

"Norma, be a petal and bring out the Smalls, will you?" said Mrs Mahoosive. She nodded towards a wide cupboard with a rusting padlock in the corner of the class.

"No!" I blurted. We couldn't bash *real Smalls*. Could we?

Everyone stared at me.

"What was that, sweetie?" said the teacher.

"No ... no ... no..." I said over and over. My skin turned as cold as ice cream. Whichever poor Smalls these giants had captured and locked in the cupboard, I had to save them.

The class raised their clubs.

And I fainted.

Chapter six

Stomping

I came to with a splutter.

Had the giants bashed me?

Was I dead?

It would be just my luck to die on my first day.

Something tickled my nose, making me sneeze. Can you sneeze when you're dead? I didn't think so.

THUNK!

DUNK!

CLUNK!

I flinched. Huge black boots thudded around my head. My class charged in circles, swinging their clubs. I scrunched my eyes closed again. Any second now, I knew those clubs would swipe *me*.

SWISH!

CRACK!

SMACK!

A minute later, I still wasn't dead.

I opened my eyes a fraction.

The giants weren't bashing me. Or any Smalls.

They were plunging their clubs into…

…a load of old scarecrows! That's right, big straw scarecrows with outstretched arms and floppy hats. The kind you find in fields to scare off pesky, pooing, crop-gobbling birds. Today, twelve stubby scarecrows were lined up in the middle of our classroom … and getting an absolute clobbering.

I almost laughed with relief. Except I was lying on the floor, covered in scarecrow straw. And NOT A SINGLE GIANT seemed to care. Not even the teacher. Which meant I was alive, but I hadn't made any friends.

The three ear-blowing bells clanged again.

DING!

DANG!

DUNG!

The class flung their clubs back on the rack and lumbered straight over me to the door.

Only Walloping stayed behind.

"Gets up sleepy head!" he chuckled. "You doesn't want to miss Group Grunting!"

At least one giant was still talking to me.

Walloping held out his huge sweaty hand to help me up.

I grabbed it, my hand squelching into his … and

flew straight over his head and into a half-bashed scarecrow.

"Woahhh," said Walloping. He stared at his sausagey fingers like they had magic powers. "I is getting super strong. You feels light as feathers!"

Uh oh.

Giants aren't supposed to feel light as feathers. Was Walloping going to guess I was secretly a Small on stilts? I had to act fast.

"Wowee!" I said, untangling myself from the scarecrow. "You're right, Walloping. You're the strongest giant I've ever met!" I pulled my best I'm-really-impressed-and-compared-to-you-I'm-not-actually-as-heavy-as-a-peanut face. Walloping beamed at me and went back to staring at his hands. I'd fooled him. For now.

I wobbled after Walloping to our next lesson.

Group Grunting was loads better than bashing, even though my grunts were more like *squeaks*. At least the handkerchief-waving was easy.

Baking class wasn't too bad either (it's just a shame we were grinding pretend Small bones into bread flour).

But Stomping was *impossible*.

A giant's guide to grunting.

1. Pull up your grunting socks.
2. Take a very deep breath.
3. Bend your knees.
4. Hold your arms out wide, waving a grunting handkerchief in each hand.
5. Stand up slowly, letting your breath out in a great big **grunt**.
6. Repeat.

Just imagine the heaviest thing you can think of.

No, heavier than that…

…*even* heavier.

Okay, good. Now imagine that a hippopotamus with a grand piano is carrying the heaviest thing you can think of. And the hippo, the piano and the heaviest thing you can think of all plonk themselves on *the ends of your feet*.

That's what it feels like to wear a giant pair of iron-bottomed stomping boots.

"Why isn't you moving?" said Walloping, as he and the rest of the class thudded up and down the room in surprisingly straight lines.

THUD.

46

THUD.

THUD.

I swung my arms forwards and back. Maybe it would look more like I was marching and less like I was standing COMPLETELY STILL.

"Owww!" snivelled Lumbering Turnip. He stopped halfway through his second lap of the classroom, grabbed his left foot and crashed around on one leg. "Miss, Walloping's stomped on my foot. Again!" he said.

At least I wasn't the only one having trouble. Walloping was stomping – but he wasn't sticking to the lines.

"Look where you're going, Walloping Toenail!" snapped Mrs Mahoosive from the back of the class.

"I tries," said Walloping. "But every time I stomps, I daydreams about stomping through the unstomped swamp paths. I wants to hear the Moaning Marsh with my own ears. I wants to sniff the Stinking Sink Pits with my own nose. I wants to climb the Vampire Mountains and clamber into the werewolves' caves." Walloping folded his arms. "I doesn't wants to stomp in straight lines. I wants to stomp over the world!"

Listening to Walloping made *me* want to stomp all over the world too. If I could only lift my feet.

"Ughhhh," groaned the whole class.

"**Not this again,**" said Mrs Mahoosive, shaking her head. "**How many times must I tell you? Giants don't travel. We're tall enough to see the world from right here. Walloping Toenail, if you stomp on another giant today, I'm sending you straight to the Headteacher.**" Mrs Mahoosive looked fierce.

"Sorry Miss," said Walloping. He hung his head so low his top hat fell off.

I was still panting and puffing, trying to drag my feet even the tiniest bit around the room when...

Crunch!

Walloping's foot landed on *my* stomping boot.

"Miss, Miss, Walloping's done it again!" cried Norma Enormous – who'd already done more laps than the whole class put together. "He'll never be a perfect stomper like me. Go on Harvey, tell Mrs Mahoosive what happened!"

Of course, I hadn't felt a thing when Walloping's big foot landed on me. My real feet were halfway up my stilts.

"Tell! Tell! Tell!" said the rest of the class, stomping their feet even harder. "Send Walloping to the Headteacher!"

This was tricky.

I wanted to make friends. And if I told on Walloping, I could make ten new friends in one go.

But so far, Walloping was the only giant who'd been nice to me.

Walloping's eyes filled with tears.

I grinned at him. "No, Mrs Mahoosive, Walloping hasn't stomped on me. Everything's fine," I said.

The class groaned. They went back to stomping up and down, but with a bit less energy than before.

Mrs Mahoosive stared at the Walloping-shaped footprint on my completely crushed stomping boot. "**Hmm,**" she said, peering at me over the top of her purple glasses. "**Okay. But I've got my eyes on you too, Harvey Small.**"

The teacher didn't have time to say anything else because…

DING!

DANG!

DUNG!

The nerve-wringing, ear-thumping bells were

back. (They made me jump so high I managed two whole steps in my stomping boots!)

"Dinnertime! Last one to the dining hall's a two-eyed cyclops!" cried Jumbolina. The class tore off their boots and charged for the door.

"Thanks," said Walloping. "The others wails when I stamps on them. But your feet is as super strong as my hands," he said. "Where does you learn to have such strong feet? Is your Ma and Pa boulder crushers? I hears you needs huge, strong feet to crush all the boulders that builds our stomping stadiums."

"Err, yes! That's exactly what they do!" I fibbed. "They're *always* crushing things. It's why I don't move much in stomping class. I don't want to show off about how strong my feet are. If I stomped too hard, I'd probably stomp right through the floor," I said, feeling pleased with my excuse.

Walloping's whole face folded into a frown.

Uh oh. Maybe I'd gone too far. He didn't believe me after all.

His body shook, slowly at first, then faster and faster until the buttons of his dungarees popped off and his stomach *ROARRRRRRRRRRRed!* I wobbled backwards, clamping my hands over my ears. For one terrifying moment, I thought he was going to explode.

Walloping laughed. "You is so funny! It's like you has never seen a hungry giant before!" he said.

I smiled. I wasn't going to tell him I hadn't.

Free of my heavier-than-a-hippo-with-a-piano-carrying-a-heavy-thing stomping boots, I followed my almost-friend to the dining hall.

I crossed my fingers giant spaghetti bolognese would be on the menu.

Chapter seven

Swamp Fish and Bogweed Sandwiches

The stench in the giants' dining hall was so strong I could actually *see* it.

A stinky green steam swept along the floor. It circled my head, stinging my nostrils with the smell of swamp weed and sludge. And it clung to two long, creaking tables that ran down the side of the hall. They bent under the weight of piles of sandwiches.

There was no spaghetti bolognese in sight.

"Swamp fish and bogweed! My favourite!" said Walloping. He grabbed a sandwich that was as big as a full loaf of bread. Something grey and shiny oozed out of it. Walloping took a bite and dropped down next to me at the end of the bench.

BOIIIIINNNNNNGGGGG!

The weight of Walloping's bottom lifted the bench like a seesaw. And I flew, face-first, into a huge pile of soggy, fishy sandwiches.

Squelch!

"Oh boy, oh boy, you is really hungry!" laughed Walloping.

The other giants didn't laugh.

They lurched towards me. "New boy's eating all the dinner. Stop him!" they hollered. The giants pulled sandwiches out of my hair, my pockets and even my armpits. They grabbed and gobbled and gobbled and grabbed.

Five seconds later, I was lying face down on an almost empty lunch table.

I peeled a last oozing sandwich off my cheek and wobbled back to Walloping.

If I wanted to fit in, I should probably eat the sandwich. I took a big bite.

I gagged.

The bogweed was bitter, the fish was slimy …

even the butter tasted like sprouts. How could giants complain about Smalls snacking on a bogey or two when they had *this* for dinner? I tried nibbling the crust instead.

"Doesn't you likes it?" said Walloping, looking sadly at the pile of crumbs that had been his sandwich only seconds ago. "It's fresh from the Stinking, Sinking Swamp. Isn't it what you eats where you lives? I finds the *Big Book for Explorers* in the library. But it doesn't say giants lives anywhere else." He gave a heavy sigh. "I wants to see the world! Ma says the world is too small and narrow for giants. But I is an explorer!" Walloping pulled crumpled sheets of paper out of every one of his pockets. He'd drawn wobbly maps of the school's vast grounds on all of them.

"These are great!" I said, picking up the maps. If I read them slowly, maybe I wouldn't have to eat any more.

"Eat up!" said Walloping, pulling the maps away.

Maybe not.

I braced myself for a second bite.

Walloping licked his lips.

It gave me an idea.

I held my soggy sandwich out to Walloping. "Where

I come from, giants *always* give food to their friends,"
I said. "Would you like my sandwich?"

Walloping's mouth fell open.

Please take it, oh please take it, I thought.

Walloping's mouth opened some more. A dollop
of dribble splatted onto the dining table. Then he
grabbed the sandwich and scoffed the lot.

Walloping smacked his lips and turned to me. His
voice wobbled. "N-n-no one ever s-s-shares food with
Walloping," he said. "Or reads my maps … or helps
me in class, like you did
in Stomping." He blew
his nose loudly on
the nearest

tablecloth, sending piles of empty plates crashing onto the floor.

Weren't they good things? I thought he was going to cry. I was about to say 'sorry' when Walloping looked me in the eyes. "You is my best friend," he said. And I forgot about fainting. I forgot about flying into fish sandwiches. I stopped worrying about being stomped on. None of it mattered, because I had a best friend!

I knew all about being a third or fourth best friend. It happened loads. But I'd never stayed in one school long enough to be someone's BEST friend before. I wished I had a giant face to fit my grin on. I looked at Walloping. *His* face was covered in fish, bogweed and dribble. I didn't care. From now on Walloping was MY BEST FRIEND and he could eat whatever he liked.

Mum was right. Joining giant school was a brilliant idea.

I was so happy, that I hadn't noticed the strange sound coming from the courtyard.

CLICKETY.

CLACKETY.

CLACK.

The giants jumped to their feet.

CLICKETY.

CLACKETY.

CLACK.

They smoothed their hair, brushed crumbs off their dungarees and fixed smiles to their faces.

CLICKETY.

CLACKETY.

CLACK...

...BANG!

A shadow fell across the entire dining hall.

I craned my head upwards ... and gasped.

"**GOOD EATING, GIFTED GIANTS**," came a booming voice from the giant towering over us.

"G-g-good eating Madame Bogbrush," snivelled the hall full of giants.

So *this* was the Headteacher.

And she looked angry.

Very angry.

Monday's dinner menu

Swamp fish and bogweed sandwiches

*

Beans on toasted fungus

*

Algae and live tadpole broth

*

Sink pit surprise

*

Turnips

*

Steaming mud pies

Chapter eight

Bad News

Madame Bogbrush stood in the middle of the dining hall, glaring at us. The Headteacher was so huge, she reminded me of the 100-year-old oak tree in Smallington Park. Or she would have done, if the oak tree had a pinched nose, steely eyes and shiny red shoes with high heels … made of meat pounders.

"The Headteacher has an allergic reaction to some beans when she is little," whispered Walloping. "Now she is as big as the school!"

I nodded. I decided to give our next dinner course (beans on toasted fungus) a miss.

"GIFTED GIANTS, I HAVE SOME BAD NEWS," boomed the Headteacher. She stomped her feet as she said 'bad.' Every giant in the hall jumped.

Quite a few of them snivelled.

"I HAVE RECEIVED A LETTER FROM THE BEASTLY SCHOOL BOARD. AN INSPECTOR WILL BE COMING TO VISIT." The Headteacher's voice whooshed through the hall with the force of a whirlwind, blowing down the younger giants like skittles. But an inspection didn't sound too bad. We'd had one at Small-Near-the-Hill Juniors last year.

"IF WE FAIL THE INSPECTION, I MUST CLOSE THE SCHOOL. FOREVER," said Madame Bogbrush.

"Huh?" said the giants, scratching their heads.

Forever? Inspectors are supposed to help schools,

not close them. Surely we'd pass. This was a school for *gifted* giants.

"WE *WILL* PASS THIS INSPECTION," said Madame Bogbrush.

See? Nothing to worry about.

"IF WE DON'T, I'LL STOMP ON EACH AND EVERY ONE OF YOU. EVEN IF YOU HAVEN'T BROKEN MY RULES."

I gulped. Being a Small was definitely against the rules. I edged behind Walloping.

Madame Bogbrush spotted me.

"YOU THERE, THE MARCHING ONE. DO YOU NEED THE TOILET?"

My cheeks burned hotter than every torch on the castle walls. I wished everyone would stop asking me that.

"THERE'LL BE NO GOING TO THE TOILET WHEN THE INSPECTOR ARRIVES. THE SMELL COULD RUIN OUR SCORES," she boomed.

Madame Bogbrush bent down. Her saucer-sized eyes examined me from top hat to toes.

I couldn't let the Headteacher see I wasn't a giant.

I couldn't be stomped on. Not now I had a best friend.

It was time to defend myself.

"I don't need the toilet!" I said, loudly this time. I remembered the fib Mum told Mr Ogg. "I'm a Country Giant. This is how we stand."

No one spoke.

The Headteacher's enormous eyes fell on my very small hands.

"And my hands are small so I can pick vegetables," I said.

Madame Bogbrush raised her right foot. The silver spikes under her meat-pounding high heel were horribly close to my head.

I kept talking.

"No, not vegetables!" I said. I struggled to think of something giants like. "Smalls!" I cried. "I use my small hands to pick out Smalls' eyeballs! Or, I would. If I ever met one. Which I haven't. Because I don't know any. Because I live with Country Giants, not Smalls."

Madame Bogbrush lowered her foot.

But I didn't stop.

"And I always march because I'm always ready to ... STOMP on Smalls. If I meet them. Which I haven't," I added.

"Yeah! Stomp on Smalls! Stomp on Smalls!" roared the giants. They pounded their hairy fists on the tables, sending half-gobbled dishes of beans on toasted fungus flying across the hall.

The Headteacher nodded. "**GOOOOOOOD**," she said, standing back up.

I smiled. I'd done it. Even the Headteacher thought I was a giant! I was going to fit in after all. "**BUT THERE'LL BE NO STOMPING ON SMALLS WHEN THE INSPECTOR ARRIVES. THE BEASTLY SCHOOL BOARD DOESN'T LIKE IT. IN FACT, WE NEED A WHOLE NEW TIMETABLE.**"

Madame Bogbrush threw a pile of poster-sized timetables on top of us. I grabbed one.

"**THE INSPECTOR SAYS SHE'LL BE JUDGING OUR PERFORMANCE. SO, WE'LL PUT ON A BRILLIANT END OF TERM SHOW FOR THE MUMS AND DADS. IT'LL BE THE BEST PERFORMANCE THE SWAMP HAS EVER SEEN.**"

Performance? When an inspector came to my last school, they wanted to know if we were good at things like maths and science and sitting quietly.

Timetable				
Monday	Tuesday	Wednesday	Thursday	Friday
Footwork for first timers	Ballet: basic stretches	Arts and crafts (mending tutus)	Double ballroom dancing: level 0	Smiling and stepping at the same time: theory
Twisting and shouting	Future studies	Disco dancing duets	Double ballroom dancing: level 0	Smiling and stepping at the same time: practice
Stepping (a 10-step masterclass)	Country dancing for dummies	Maths	Tango training	Swamp gardening
Baking	Tap dancing for total beginners	Cancan dancing: kick-starter class	Performance skills: level 10	Waltz work
Dinner	Dinner	Dinner	Dinner	Dinner

Not show business. Doing a show's okay though (as long as no one breaks a leg). When I was Second Lamppost in my last school play, Mum said she was so proud she could burst. If I got a good part, I bet Mum and Dad would both come and watch me.

65

Maybe they'd even make up and Dad would live with us again.

I joined the giants, cheering and stomping my feet.

Walloping frowned at his timetable. "Ballet dancing? I is a giant. I does stomping and clomping. I does not do ballet dancing! What *is* ballet dancing? Is it something Country Giants does?"

"AH, YES," said Madame Bogbrush, answering before I could say anything. "THE INSPECTOR SAYS YOU MUST STRETCH YOURSELVES. THERE'S NOT ENOUGH STRETCHING IN GRUNTING. SO, WE'RE PUTTING ON A DANCING PERFORMANCE INSTEAD."

The giants scratched their heads. They looked even more confused than usual. I was confused too. I didn't think dancing was the kind of stretching the school inspector had in mind.

"MRS MAHOOSIVE WILL WORK OUT THE DETAILS," said the Headteacher.

A book called *Dancing for Absolute Beginners* crashed down at the teacher's feet.

"NOW GET SOME SLEEP. THE INSPECTOR ARRIVES TOMORROW. I EXPECT YOU TO DANCE PERFECTLY."

Oh no.

I'm a terrible dancer. Dad says I have two left feet. Now I'd have two left feet *on stilts*! What if the whole school failed the inspection because of me?

For the attention of Madame Bogbrush

Just because your school's in the middle of a stinky, sinky swamp, you can't hide from us.

Our Chief Inspector, Ms Sugar Plum is on her way.

Kindly remember that according to the Beastly School Code, a good school must:
- stretch its students
- prepare students for the future
- teach students to spell.

Nothing less than an excellent performance will do.

Fail and we're shutting you down.
Forever.

Lots of love and kisses,
The Beastly School Board

Chapter nine

Scary Stories

It was finally bedtime. And I wouldn't need to worry about school inspectors or ballet dancing until morning.

Walloping led me down a seemingly endless maze of cold twisty corridors. "Keeps away from that corridor there," he said, waving towards an even darker corner of the castle. It shimmered with slime. "That's Kevin's."

"Kevin?" I asked. Kevin didn't sound like a giant's name.

Two eyes on stalks blinked at me in the darkness and a rubbery mouth gnashed. I leaped backwards.

"Kevin's the school slug. Sort of a pet. Sort of a

big, slimy troublemaker," he giggled. "We rescues him from the beak of a baby Swamp Flapper when he was just the size of a sausage. But we didn't knows how much he'd grow!"

Kevin made a slurping noise. I wasn't good with pets. I had a horrible feeling this one wanted to eat me.

"And this is where we sleeps!" said Walloping, opening a door that was a bit too close to Kevin for my liking. I looked back into the corridor. Kevin's ginormous eye tentacles were still waving at me. I dashed into the dorm.

A whiff of bog broth and sweaty socks hit me so hard my eyes watered.

"Here's your bunk, best friend! Right under mine!" said Walloping with a dribbly grin. I grinned back, trying not to breathe too deeply. Our dorm had a cold stone floor like the rest of the castle, but it was covered in piles of old pants, scattered pounding gloves and forgotten mugs that probably weren't meant to be furry. Gifted giants *weren't* gifted at being tidy.

The dorm walls were covered with posters of famous giants. I peered at the picture closest to our bunk. A pair of hairy arms gripped a club that was so big you could barely see the giant behind it.

"That's Lady Clout. She's five time bashing and clobbering champion! She be my favourite giant … aparts from you, of course," said Walloping.

I smiled. I was glad I wouldn't have to do any clobbering tomorrow.

The day had felt as loooong as the castle corridors. I heaved my stilts onto the bed and pulled my extra-long pyjamas on under the covers. All I wanted to do was sleep.

"Who's got tonight's story?" said Gallumphing, rubbing his huge hands together. "And make it a scary one!"

I yawned, heaving myself up. I was tired, but I liked stories. Mum never lets me listen to anything scary at bedtime.

"I've got one!" said Jumbolina, bouncing on her top bunk. "It's about the giant with the haunted bashing club. He found it at the bottom of the swamp and…"

"Heard it," yawned Gallumphing. "Who's got another?"

"My Pa tells a terrifying story," said Norma Enormous. "It's about all the terrible things that happen to giants who FAIL their bashing and grunting exams," she added. Maybe that's why Norma tried so hard to be best in every lesson.

"BORING!" said Jumbolina.

I had a story.

"Country Giants are only scared of one thing," I said.

The giants leaned forward in their bunks.

CREAAAAAAK. TWANG!

"The Unspeakable Circus," I said.

"No!" said Walloping, hanging his head down from the bunk above me. "We is scared of it too."

That was strange. I knew the circus was scary for Smalls. I'd heard stomach-knottingly unspeakable things about it since I was tiny. How did those stories make it all the way out here?

"I reads about it in my *Big Book for Explorers*," said Walloping.

"We heard the Unspeakable Circus has skeleton lions, brought back from the dead! You can see right through them. But they'll still chomp your head off!" said the class twins, Maxi and Maximus Maximus, huddling together.

I'd heard that too. I pulled my covers up to my neck.

"They say the evil Ring Mistress is a Small. She saws swamp creatures in half and doesn't stick them back together again!" said Jumbolina, clutching her cuddly toy-bashing club.

Everyone
shuddered.

"That's why
we bashes all the horrible,
bogey-eating Smalls!" said Walloping.

The giants nodded, thumping the sides of their
bunk beds.

"Bash the Smalls! Bash the Smalls!" they chanted.

I felt like I'd been blasted in the face with a water
pistol. My best friend couldn't think *all* Smalls were
like the Ring Mistress from the Unspeakable Circus.
Could he?

A noise came from our bedroom window. It was
open.

Hisssss.

I jumped so high I hit the bottom of Walloping's mattress.

Hisssssss, came the noise again.

Two yellow eyes appeared at the window. And tiny claws. And flapping, pointy ears. I'd seen the creature before. It was a swamp goblin.

I pulled the covers over my nose.

There'ssss been rumours acrosssss the sssssswamp, hissed the goblin. *Zombie clowns visits the bogeyman school. Sssssteals their best bogey in the night. Nowhere is sssssssafe.*

The giants gasped. A few sobs squeaked out around the dorm.

Zombie clowns scared me even more than swamp goblins or school slugs.

Gallumphing leaped from his bunk, fists clenched. Was he going to grab the goblin? Or demand to hear more? Before he got close, the goblin stuck her tongue out, blew a massive raspberry and scuttled into the night.

There was only one thought buzzing through my brain. "I've heard the zombie clowns *eat* lost children,"

I blurted. Then I looked at the giants and immediately wished I'd kept my big mouth shut.

We were quaking so much the bunk beds shook. We'd be too scared to sleep. Our dancing would be even worse tomorrow. We'd fail the school inspection. And it would all be my fault! Then the Beastly School Board would shut us down and probably feed us to the clowns.

"It's okay," I said, trying to sound reassuring.

"Is it?" whimpered Walloping. He hung his head over the bunk again. He'd gone whiter than the bedsheets.

"Of course. We're in the world's biggest, strongest castle, right in the middle of the Stinking, Sinking Swamp. There's *no way* the Unspeakable Circus could get here. It's impossible."

"Y-y-yes, impossible," agreed Norma Enormous.

"There's no way at all," said Gallumphing.

"None," agreed Jumbolina.

No one said anything after that.

When I was sure everyone else was asleep, I felt in my suitcase for Mr Snout. At times like this I bet even the bravest people on the planet reach for a paw. I squeezed my favourite teddy and tried not to think about evil ring mistresses, skeleton lions and zombie clowns who steal children in the night. They couldn't get us here. Everything would be alright.

Probably.

Chapter ten

Stretching

I saw the flying clipboard before I saw the school inspector. The clipboard seemed to be floating down the corridor all by itself. Until it clattered down on Lumbering Turnip's head with a *thunk*.

"Straighten your top hat, boy," said a small, sharp voice.

"Ow! Who said that?" moaned Lumbering.

"I did, blockhead ... Me. Ms Sugar Plum," said the voice.

Behind the giant-sized clipboard, a fairy with plum-coloured wings and a fluffy pink dress flapped furiously. She reminded me of a stick of candyfloss. A *grumpy* stick of candyfloss.

"The school inspector's an Extra Small!" gasped Walloping. "I has never met an Extra Small before! I hears they live inside the petals of marsh marigolds. But they is too small to see from the castle grounds, even if your eyes are as big as the Headteacher's."

The inspector was the size of my hand. For once I almost felt *big*.

Mrs Mahoosive hurried us into the classroom. She smiled, but when she pushed her purple spectacles up her nose, her hand shook.

"I see you've met Ms Sugar Plum," she said. **"The inspector will watch our lessons for a while. Nothing to worry about. She's judging me, not you."**

"Wrong! I'm judging *them*, dodo. Got to see if they're as gifted as you say," said Ms Sugar Plum, whacking Gallumphing Doorknob on the side of the head with her clipboard.

"Hey!" he cried.

"Ms Sugar Plum thinks a good school should stretch its students," said Mrs Mahoosive. **"Which, of course, we always do,"** she laughed and pushed her spectacles up again. **"Stretch, stretch, stretch. That's all we do, really. We stretch up, we stretch down, we stretch sideways,"** Mrs Mahoosive flapped her arms as she talked, trying to show off her own stretchiness.

We gawped at her.

When Norma put her hand up, beginning, "But Miss, we don't…" Mrs Mahoosive talked straight over her, "**Mr Ogg, we're ready for you.**"

CLOMP.

SQUEAK.

CLOMP.

SQUEAK!

Mr Ogg wheeled a squeaky clothes rail into the classroom.

It was full of sludge-brown leotards with gold sparkles.

And tutus.

And tights.

They were the kinds of clothes Mum kept hidden at the back of the wardrobe.

"***SMALL*** clothes!" shrieked the giants.

"They're too twinkly!" cried Walloping, covering his eyes.

"Let's bash 'em!" said Jumbolina, running forwards with her club.

Ms Sugar Plum tutted and scribbled something on her clipboard.

"**Don't be silly,**" said Mrs Mahoosive. "**These are *your* clothes. For dancing. And stretching. They're** the clothes you *always* wear, remember. Put your clubs away and get dressed."

Now I had a real problem. I couldn't change into dance clothes with the class watching. Everyone would see my stilts!

That's when my best friend pulled a tutu off the clothes rail. He pushed it over his head, until he was wearing it like a collar. "What's this for?" he asked.

Walloping was a genius! I pulled a tutu round my neck, too.

"That's not how you wear them, wally," said Ms Sugar Plum, clonking Walloping and me with her clipboard.

"Yes, it is," I said. "It's how giants *always* wear them, isn't it, Mrs Mahoosive?" There was no way the teacher would want to look silly in front of the inspector.

Mrs Mahoosive smiled. "Of course, it is. Quick everyone, put on your dancing collars!"

Soon, the entire class had tutus round their necks. And no one had taken their dungarees off.

Norma Enormous stretched a pair of glittery tights up her arms, too. "I know I'll be the best at dancing," she said. "Just as soon as I work out what it is."

Norma was best at everything. At least, she thought she was.

When the inspector wasn't looking, Mrs Mahoosive read from the first page

of *Dancing for Absolute Beginners*.

"**Now, stand in a line and stick your arms out to the side,**" she said.

It should have been an easy move, even for me. But it's hard to see properly when you're wearing a big tutu skirt round your neck.

"**One, two, three: stretch!**" cried Mrs Mahoosive.

"Oof!"

"Argh!"

"Ow!" cried the class.

The giants flung their heavy arms out so enthusiastically they punched each other on the nose! Walloping walloped my nose so hard it started bleeding.

"Owwww!" I cried.

My best friend looked at me in horror, before turning a bright shade of green and collapsing on the floor.

He wasn't the only one.

The class gawped at the blood dribbling into my tutu. Half of them turned green and fainted too.

I stumbled around, holding my stinging nose (it felt as big and swollen as a real giant's nose).

Ms Sugar Plum tutted.

"Fizzling fairy dust! You're getting blood on my dress, bozo!" cried the inspector, wiping her pink dress and whacking me with her clipboard.

All the while, Mrs Mahoosive flicked through the pages of *Dancing for Absolute Beginners*, shaking her head. "**Oh dear!**" she said to the angry, nosebleed-splattered inspector. "**We're normally so much better at stretching than this.**"

Ms Sugar Plum tutted. "I doubt it," she said, scribbling on her clipboard.

I gulped. We'd failed our first inspection test.

And it was all my fault.

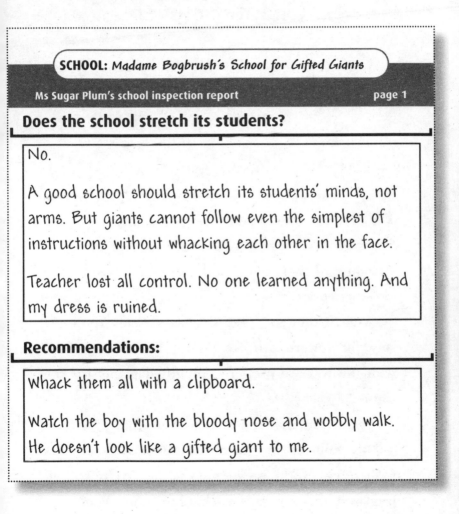

SCHOOL: Madame Bogbrush's School for Gifted Giants

Ms Sugar Plum's school inspection report   page 1

Does the school stretch its students?

No.

A good school should stretch its students' minds, not arms. But giants cannot follow even the simplest of instructions without whacking each other in the face.

Teacher lost all control. No one learned anything. And my dress is ruined.

Recommendations:

Whack them all with a clipboard.

Watch the boy with the bloody nose and wobbly walk. He doesn't look like a gifted giant to me.

Chapter eleven

Preparing for the Future

My bloody nose was still stinging. My classmates were still green and groaning. And Ms Sugar Plum was still tutting. The school inspector straightened her tiara and flapped towards the classroom door.

"Wait! Don't go!" said Mrs Mahoosive. "You must stay for Future Studies. You'll be so impressed with the way we prepare our gifted giants for the future."

"Hmph," said the fairy, shaking her head.

"It's one of my favourite lessons," said Mrs Mahoosive. "Nothing ever goes wrong. We're so well prepared, we even have a school fortune teller."

"You've got a school fortune teller?" I whispered to Walloping. I was impressed, even if Ms Sugar Plum wasn't.

"Yeah, most swamp schools do. But she's boring," whispered Walloping. "Exciting things don't happen here. All she does is write us letters to say if the swamp's getting too bubbly or if we needs to bash any swamp goblins. We hardly ever studies her now."

"No whispering!" tutted the fairy, scribbling something too small to read on her clipboard.

The whole class glared at Walloping and me. Everything I did seemed to upset the inspector.

Mrs Mahoosive pulled a pile of envelopes out of her flowery purple handbag. "**Okay, class, let's *prepare for the future* like we always do, by reading the fortune teller's predictions for this half-term. Grab a desk and sit down.**"

Norma heaved desks and chairs out of the class cupboard, throwing them at the giants. In seconds our ballet studio became an ordinary classroom again. We might have failed stretching. But preparing for the future sounded nice and easy. And a little bit exciting, too.

Mrs Mahoosive opened the first envelope. I leaned

forward in my seat. I'd never heard a real prediction before.

"Expect an EXPLOSION..." she began.

Gallumphing yawned.

Ms Sugar Plum tutted.

"Shh!" I said. This was the most important lesson we'd had since I arrived. If the school was about to explode, I needed to know about it.

Mrs Mahoosive continued.

"Expect an explosion *of colour* in the swamp as autumn sets in."

Oh. I relaxed a bit.

"Next week, prepare for an ATTACK..."

Walloping doodled maps of the swamp in his notebook.

Ms Sugar Plum tutted.

Why wasn't Walloping listening? This was serious.

"...an attack of moss on the school steps," said Mrs Mahoosive. "They'll be extra slippery."

I relaxed a bit more.

Jumbolina lay her head on the desk.

Ms Sugar Plum tutted.

Mrs Mahoosive raised her voice. I think she was trying to keep us awake to stop Ms Sugar Plum tutting. "GREAT DARKNESS…" she said, stomping her feet, "…**will come when a breeze from the east blows out the candles.**"

This wasn't the future; it was *the weather.*

Mrs Mahoosive's voice got so loud the castle windows rattled in their frames. I stuck my fingers in my ears.

Ms Sugar Plum tutted.

By the time she reached the last prediction of term, Mrs Mahoosive was red-faced and bellowing. "**DANGER … WILL COME FROM ONE WHO'S NOT WHO THEY SAY. AN INNOCENT GIANT WILL BE STOLEN AWAY. BEWARE THE UNCHOSEN ONE!**"

I jolted in my seat. *That* didn't sound like the weather.

"Huh?" said the class. Everyone was wide awake now.

Ms Sugar Plum tutted.

"**Oh,**" said Mrs Mahoosive. She looked surprised to see us staring at her. "**That can't be right.**" She squinted at the letter and read it again. "***Grave* danger will come from one who's not who they say. An innocent giant will be stolen away. Beware the Unchosen One.**"

Grave danger? That was even worse! Walloping jumped out of his seat. "DANGER! DANGER! Who's missing? Has anyone been takens yet?" He charged between the desks counting us all.

"Grab the bashing clubs!" yelled Jumbolina, pushing her desk over.

"And the stomping boots!" said Gallumphing, jumping on top of his.

"And the pounding gloves!" said Lumbering Turnip, pounding his desk so hard it split in two.

Ms Sugar Plum scribbled furiously on her clipboard.

"Wait, there must be some mistake!" said Mrs Mahoosive. She flipped the prediction over and turned it upside down, looking for answers. She didn't find any.

"We should never go anywhere by ourselves," said Gallumphing. "Then if the Unchosen One tries to steal us, someone will tell the teachers."

"We should call our mums," wailed Lumbering, snivelling into his sleeve.

"We should bash anyone who doesn't look like us," said Jumbolina. "They'll be the Unchosen One!"

"Yeah!" the class agreed. A few of them glanced at

Ms Sugar Plum, who tutted. Then they looked at my small hands. I pushed them inside my pockets.

Walloping saw the looks too. He thumped a heavy arm around my shoulder. "Don't worry, best friend," he said. "The Unchosen One won't be a Country Giant. To steal one of us, they'll has to be someone really terrible…"

I nodded.

"Someone awful and scary and mean…" Walloping went on.

I nodded again. *Of course*, it wasn't going to be me.

"…I bet they'll be a Small," he said.

Oh.

I deflated like a balloon without a knot. Having a best friend was great. But it was hard to forget the teeny tiny possibility Walloping might bash me to bits if he knew I was a Small.

"Maybe I should shut the school down right now," said Ms Sugar Plum, looking gleeful.

"No!" said Mrs Mahoosive. "I'll talk to Madame Bogbrush. I'm sure the prediction's wrong."

I didn't think the prediction was wrong.

I thought Walloping was right.

I'm not who I say I am.

I'm a Small.

And I'm bad news.

If I could split my parents up with a football boot, I bet I could steal a giant. Even if I didn't want to.

I must be the Unchosen One.

SCHOOL: *Madame Bogbrush's School for Gifted Giants*

Ms Sugar Plum's school inspection report   page 2

Does the school prepare students for the future?

Absolutely not.

A good school gives its students the skills to face life's challenges.

At the slightest hint of grave danger, the giants snivel like babies and run around asking for bashing clubs.

Recommendations:

Whack them all with a clipboard.

Keep watching the whispering boy with the small hands, wobbly walk and bloody nose. He was suspiciously interested in the lesson. Can he really be a giant?

Chapter twelve

Saving the School

It's a lot to take in, right? Is your head ready to explode? Well just imagine how mine was feeling! Here I was, a Small on stilts, still trying to fool everyone that I was a giant. Trying to impress the grumpy school inspector after spewing nose blood all over her dress. And then I found out I WAS GOING TO STEAL A GIANT AND BRING GRAVE DANGER TO THE SCHOOL!!!

I didn't care what Mrs Mahoosive said. I'm bad news, so I knew the fortune teller's prediction was true. Madame Bogbrush knew it, too. But instead of calming the class down, she smashed into our first tap dancing lesson and said (well, boomed), "**STOP**

MAKING A FUSS IN FRONT OF THE INSPECTOR. WE'RE ONLY LOSING ONE OF YOU. I DOUBT IT WILL BE ANYONE TRULY GIFTED. GET BACK TO DANCING!"

Then she *CLICKETY*, *CLACKETY*, *CLACKED* away again.

I braced myself for more panic from the class.

"Well, we *are* the most gifted giants in school," said Norma Enormous, twirling an extra-long bashing club. She was using it as a tap-dancing cane.

"Yeah, we can look after

ourselves," said Gallumphing, balling his hands into fists.

Jumbolina nodded, straightening her top hat. "It'll probably be someone in Master Massive's class that gets bashed ... I mean, stolen."

Ms Sugar Plum's tiny eyes lit up at the mention of *even less* gifted students than us. The school inspector and her humungous clipboard flitted away.

And that was it. Panic over. For everyone apart from me. Because I was the only one who knew what a danger I was. Someone had to stop me. Unfortunately, it looked like that someone, was me. "Walloping, I don't want *anyone* to be stolen, even if they're in Master Massive's class," I said, as we fastened our stomping boots. (Mrs Mahoosive decided wearing iron weights on our feet was perfect for tap dancing.) "I think we should talk to the Fortune Teller in the Cellar."

"You can't talk to her," said Norma Enormous, tap dancing towards us. Somehow, she was already dancing in time to the music. Well, in time to Mr Ogg's very squeaky trumpet playing.

"The fortune teller hides from Smalls in a secret cellar somewhere in the school," said Norma, twirling her bashing club cane and tapping her feet. "Smalls get spooked by her predictions. Rule 387 says we're not allowed to find her. I'm the best at *not* finding her."

"Who's talking about the Fortune Teller in the Cellar?" said Mrs Mahoosive. **"Stop that at once."**

Sometimes, you can't save a school without breaking a few rules. And since stealing a giant was loads worse than finding a little old cellar, I wasn't going to let rule 387 stop me. The fortune teller had to tell me how to save the school from ... me. And I'd need my best friend's help to find her.

I know what you're thinking.

If Walloping helped me find the Fortune Teller in the Cellar, she might tell him I'm not a giant. Then I might lose my best friend and get stomped on.

But.

The school was so gigantically, ridiculously enormous, I'd never find the secret cellar without Walloping's maps. Then, I'd never know how to put a terrible stop to whatever gravely dangerous thing I was about to do.

I'd figure out how to stop the fortune teller telling on *me* once we found her.

*

For the next few days, every conversation I had with Walloping went like this:

Me: "Please help me find the Fortune Teller in the Cellar. I need your maps to explore the school."

Walloping: "But it's against the rules!"

Me: "Don't you want to save the school from grave danger?"

Walloping: "Madame Bogbrush will stomp on us!"

Three days, and a lot of persuading later, we were standing in Walloping's favourite spot. From the top of the tallest school tower, we could see right out over the swamp. If I peered hard enough, I bet I could even see all the way back to Smallington.

"That's where Ma and Pa lives," said Walloping, pointing out beyond the school's back gates. Rows of wonky rooftops clustered together. Puffs of green smoke billowed from the chimneys.

"Has you ever been to Bogeyman Bog?" Walloping asked, waving to the east where the swamp turned from green to brown and seemed to bubble more fiercely. "Or to the Vampire Mountains?" he asked, pointing at the jagged mountain range on the horizon. I shook my head.

"Oh, I wants to stomp over all of it," said Walloping.

"I doesn't just want to look at it. One day, I is going to be the world's best explorer!"

I knew this was my chance to convince Walloping to help me once and for all.

"Then won't you explore the school with me?" I said. "Pleaaaaassssssseeeeeeee?"

Walloping looked towards the Bogeyman Bog, then back at me. His mouth wobbled with worry. "Alright," he said eventually. "But only because you is my best friend."

I nodded, giving Walloping my most serious face to show I understood.

To find the cellar without the teachers catching us, we'd need to be sneakier than we'd ever been before.

*

"I doesn't know how to be sneaky!" said Walloping, tucking into his third helping of swamp stew at dinner time.

"You just have to be really, really, really quiet," I explained. "So tiptoe to the Stew Station..." (A bowl as big as seven bathtubs, filled with steaming green swamp stew.) "...and tiptoe back to me as quietly as you can," I said.

"Okay," said Walloping, knocking over the entire dining table as he stood up. I tried to look encouraging.

Walloping rolled onto his tiptoes and headed for the Stew Station.

CLOMPITY.

THUMPITY.

STOMPITY.

CLOMP.

If anything, he was louder than usual. He wobbled so much he sent tables, chairs and a few of the younger giants flying. (If he thought tiptoes were wobbly, he should try being on stilts!) "How about this?" I said. "Think about everything we do in Stomping class and ... do the opposite!"

"Got it!" said Walloping, sticking his thumbs in the air.

Off he went again.

CLOMP.

STOMPITY.

THUMPITY.

CLOMPITY.

"The opposite of stomping isn't stomping BACKWARDS!" I cried.

I sighed. Walloping's sneaking could easily get us in a lot of trouble. But it would have to do.

The next day, we tried sneaking into Master Massive's classroom. It's at the end of the longest, darkest corridor in school. It looked like a great spot to hide a secret cellar door. Unfortunately, Walloping's tiptoeing didn't go well. Instead of creeping up to the door, he lost balance and toppled into it head-first.

"**WHAT are you doing here?**" said Master Massive, peering down his exceptionally long nose at us. "**It's break time. You should be enjoying the stinking swamp air.**"

"Yes Sir, sorry Sir," we mumbled. I tried to look past the teacher and into his classroom. He slammed the door on us.

Suspicious.

Very suspicious.

"Master Massive could easily hide a cellar door in his floor," I said. But we didn't dare sneak into his classroom a second time.

"Don't worry! I'm sure we'll finds the cellar in the school kitchens," said Walloping. "I bets that's how the fortune teller gets her dinners!"

This time, we made it across the courtyard and

round the back of the dining hall without anyone spotting us.

"All we has to do is follow one of the swamp grocers up the kitchen steps and we'll gets in!" said Walloping.

For once, I thought my best friend was right.

We didn't wait long.

A stocky giant, carrying a wriggling sack, stomped towards the kitchen.

"Quick! Let's go!" I said. We dashed after the grocer and...

Donk.

Donk.

Clonk.

"Owww!"

The steps were covered in so much moss that we slipped right off them!

"What are you young'uns doing on the ground?" said the swamp grocer. **"Trying to steal a juicy three-headed swamp worm?"** He pushed his hands deep in his apron pocket and threw two worms with two too many heads

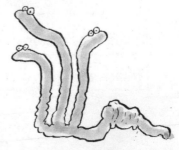

at us. I tried not to wince as the slimy creature wriggled in my lap.

"I hate seeing growing giants go hungry. Go on, gobble them up!" said the swamp grocer.

"Thank you, Sir," I said.

I closed my eyes to take a squelchy bite, when I heard a *"Tut!"*

Ms Sugar Plum, the school inspector, was staring at us.

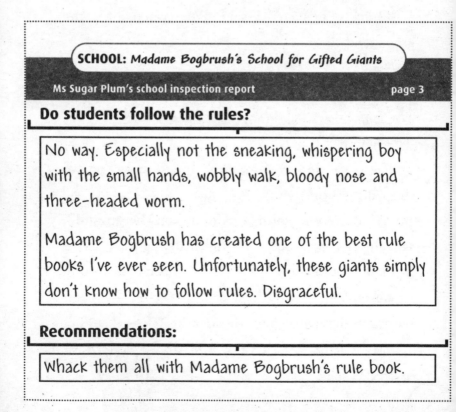

SCHOOL: *Madame Bogbrush's School for Gifted Giants*

Ms Sugar Plum's school inspection report   page 3

Do students follow the rules?

No way. Especially not the sneaking, whispering boy with the small hands, wobbly walk, bloody nose and three-headed worm.

Madame Bogbrush has created one of the best rule books I've ever seen. Unfortunately, these giants simply don't know how to follow rules. Disgraceful.

Recommendations:

Whack them all with Madame Bogbrush's rule book.

Chapter thirteen

Spellings

Ms Sugar Plum raised her clipboard and whacked Walloping and me on the head. *Hard*.

"That's for breaking Madame Bogbrush's excellent rules," said the furious fairy. "Sneaking around school. Disturbing the kitchen staff. Spoiling your dinner with three-headed snacks," she shook her head. "I'll have to put this in my inspection report," she said, scribbling on her clipboard.

Walloping's bottom lip wobbled. "But Madame Bogbrush will stomp on us!" he wailed.

"We're only trying to save the school from grave danger!" I said.

"You expect me to believe that, numbskulls?" said the fairy, whacking us again. "You're greedy little worm-gobblers. I could shut the school down for your rule-breaking!"

"No!" I cried. I'd brought bad news to plenty of schools before, but I'd never shut one down.

Walloping started sobbing.

Ms Sugar Plum tutted, then sighed.

"Fine. Save the school from grave danger before I leave…" she said. "…And I won't tell Madame Bogbrush about the sneaking. If you can't save the school, I'm telling her everything." The fairy whacked us once more with her clipboard, stuck her tongue out and flapped away.

"Oh no, oh no, oh no," said Walloping, drenching me in snot and sobs. "What if we has to go to the werewolves' school instead? I meets a werewolf once at the Swamp Schools' Summer Party. Their fur gives me sneezes!"

"Don't worry," I said. "We'll save the school. I know we will."

For the next three weeks, we didn't save the school.

Every day was the same. We spent our dance lessons kicking open doors, twirling behind curtains and rocking and rolling under rugs. We spent our breaks making too much noise to sneak anywhere without being spotted. And Ms Sugar Plum spent every lesson tutting.

I'll be honest, I was starting to panic. At this rate, we'd never find the Fortune Teller in the Cellar. I'd never know how to stop the Unchosen One (me). And Walloping and I would get stomped on by Madame Bogbrush.

Then came the cancan class.

Ms Sugar Plum and her humungous clipboard were back.

I was busy kicking my stilt legs when I saw a strange marking on the floor.

Could this be it?

Had I finally found the secret cellar door? I wobbled down to check, accidentally making Walloping trip over me. Which made Walloping accidentally kick Gallumphing Doorknob on the nose.

"Owwwwww!"

Which made Gallumphing stumble sideways into Lumbering Turnip.

"Hey!"

Which made Lumbering lunge snotty-nose-first into Norma Enormous, knocking her red feather

103

cancan hat across the room. "Great Goliaths!" she cried. "How am I supposed to give the best cancan performance if you brutes keep bashing into me?"

"Who are you calling a brute?" said Gallumphing, balling his hands into brutish fists.

The whole class was fighting, and it was all my fault! (Oh, and that mark on the floor wasn't the door. It was just a bit of old swamp weed.)

Ms Sugar Plum tutted, whacked each of us on the head with her clipboard and scribbled furiously. The big end of term performance (and Ms Sugar Plum's final inspection) was days away. Grave danger or not, if we failed the inspection, the Beastly School Board would shut down the school.

CLICKETY.

CLACKETY.

CLACK.

And things were about to get *even* worse.

Madame Bogbrush was coming.

CLICKETY.

CLACKETY.

CLACK.

She'd heard the fight.

She'd see the angry school inspector.

She was going to stomp us into sandwiches!

CLICKETY.

CLACKETY.

CLACK.

"**Quick everyone!**" said Mrs Mahoosive. She was shaking. "**Places!**"

Gallumphing dropped his fists. We made a perfect cancan line and stood, quaking by the door.

BANG!

The room went dark as midnight. Madame Bogbrush's shadow covered us all. But she didn't look angry.

A blinding white light shone through the darkness.

It was Madame Bogbrush's teeth.

She was ... smiling!

"**GOOD DANCING, GIFTED GIANTS,**" she said. "**AND HELLO MS SUGAR PLUM, HOW MARVELLOUS TO SEE YOU. I TRUST THE INSPECTION IS GOING WELL.**"

"*Hmph!*" said the fairy, shaking her clipboard.

"I HAVE GREAT NEWS ABOUT OUR SPELLINGS," said Madame Bogbrush.

I smiled. I'm a terrible dancer but I'm good at spellings. The rest of the class scratched their heads. They looked at the Headteacher blankly.

"WE'LL BE ADDING AN EXTRA SPECIAL SPELL TO OUR END OF TERM PERFORMANCE," said the Headteacher.

An extra special spell? Did she mean extra special spellings? I bet we'd have some really hard words to learn. Long words like *thesaurus* or *brachiosaurus* or *dodecahedron*. (I could spell all of those already.)

"A VANISHING SPELL!" said Madame Bogbrush, clicking her heels together.

"Huh?" said the whole class (even Ms Sugar Plum).

I grinned. 'Vanishing' was an easy word to spell.

"SAY 'HELLO' TO YOUR NEW SPELLING TEACHER," said Madame Bogbrush. She stepped aside. A small giant lurked in the doorway behind her. This giant was only just taller than me on stilts. She had a long red jacket with shiny gold buttons. She carried a whip, with an ornate handle in the shape of a lion. And she had an old wooden trunk by her side.

"Look!" said Walloping, "She has small hands, like you. I bet she be a Country Giant!"

Which was odd, since I knew Country Giants weren't real.

"**THIS IS MISTRESS RING,**" said Madame Bogbrush, smiling down at the teacher. "**SHE'S GOING TO TEACH ONE GIFTED GIANT A FINALE FOR OUR SPECIAL PERFORMANCE … A VANISHING SPELL! YOU'LL AMAZE**

MS SUGAR PLUM AND THE MUMS AND DADS
BY VANISHING FOR FIVE WHOLE MINUTES!"

"Ooooohhhh," said the whole class (even me).

Ms Sugar Plum tutted and scribbled on her clipboard. I had a feeling *magic spells* weren't what she wanted to test us on.

Mistress Ring flashed us a dazzling smile. "**Ladies and gentlemen, boys and girls...**" she began. For such a small giant, the new teacher's voice boomed.

We gawped at her.

"**I mean, giants young and old!**" she said. "**Roll up, try your luck and be terrified, um, I mean *amazed* by the magnificence of magic!**" She waved her small hands and waggled her fingers as she said 'amazed.'

Ms Sugar Plum tutted.

I looked at Walloping. His grin was even bigger than usual. We flung our hands in the air.

"I want to vanish!" cried the whole class at once.

"No, *I* want to vanish!" I shouted, surprising myself at how loud I was. Norma Enormous frowned at me.

If I learned to magically disappear, I'd be invisible. I could go back to Master Massive's classroom and search for the fortune teller's cellar. No one would see me.

Yes. Vanishing was a very good idea.

Mistress Ring reached her surprisingly short arm towards me.

"**Very well,**" she said. "**You first.**"

Are the students good at spelling?

Too early to tell. But if the Headteacher thinks she can distract me with magic tricks, she's got another thing coming.

Recommendations:

Whack Madame Bogbrush on the head with my clipboard. And a dictionary.

Keep an eye on the sneaking, whispering boy with the small hands, wobbly walk, bloody nose and three-headed worm. He seems suspiciously keen to vanish. He's probably up to no good.

Chapter fourteen

Learning to Vanish

I don't think Ms Sugar Plum liked meeting our new spelling teacher. The inspector tutted, shook her tiny head and flapped off.

Norma Enormous leaned over and whispered in my ear, "*I'll* be the best at magic, so you can forget about being in the vanishing grand finale."

I ignored her. After all, Mistress Ring had chosen *me* to vanish first.

The new teacher stared at me. Her eyes were so green, it looked like she'd coloured them with crayons.

I stared back. I wasn't scared. I was ready to

disappear, find the fortune teller and put a stop to myself (and the grave danger).

The teacher cracked her long black whip on the floor.

The class gasped.

But I didn't disappear.

"Can you juggle, boy?" Mistress Ring asked. She pulled out three shiny batons from her trunk and threw them at me. The batons clattered to the floor. I can't juggle.

"Or breathe fire?" she said, hopefully. She lit another club on a flaming torch and flung it at my head. I dodged, letting it land on *Tap Dancing for Total Beginners*. The pages sizzled.

A smile crept onto the corner of the teacher's lips. **"No matter. How would you feel if I threw knives at you?"**

"What?!" I said.

"Sharp ones," she added.

I gulped. What was she talking about? Teachers aren't allowed to throw knives! Besides, knives wouldn't help me learn a vanishing spell.

"Please Miss," said Maxi and Maximus Maximus, the class twins, "We can juggle." They grabbed four bashing clubs from the rack and pushed in front of me. They tossed the clubs up in the air and across to each other in a dizzying arc.

The teacher's eyes lit up.

"**Yes, yes,**" she murmured. "**But will I have room for both of you?**"

Room? I'd seen the stomping ground where we'd be performing. It was round the back of the castle and it stretched for miles. There was loads of room.

"I can cartwheel, Miss. I'm the best at it," said Norma Enormous. She cartwheeled straight into the juggling twins, sending them flying.

Just like that, everyone was showing off to the new teacher.

But no one was vanishing. Which meant I still had a chance.

I tapped Mistress Ring on the shoulder. "Mistress Ring, *how* do you do a vanishing spell?" I asked.

"**Ahah!**" said the teacher, flashing us another dazzling smile. She pulled a small wooden box from her trunk. It was filled with bottles of bright blue liquid.

"**This...**" she said in a dramatic whisper, "**...is my Extra Special Top-Secret Vanishing Potion. The chosen giant will drink it moments before they go on stage ... and they'll vanish before your very eyes!**"

Walloping flung his hand up. "Miss, why does the Extra Special Top-Secret Vanishing Potions have skulls on them?"

He was right. Every bottle had a creepy skull-shaped glass stopper.

Mistress Ring slammed the box shut. "**Skulls?**" she said, giving a strange, high-pitched laugh. "**They're not skulls, they're faces. *Happy faces.***"

They looked like skulls to me.

It wasn't fair. If all we needed to do was drink a potion with a skull on it, then why did it matter if I could juggle or breathe fire?

DING!

DANG!

DUNG!

Oh no. The ear-splitting, brain-boggling bells meant the lesson was already over. "Mistress Ring!" I asked as everyone charged out the door. "Could I have a bottle of vanishing potion … to practice on? I really want to be in the finale." Teachers normally love it when you ask for extra homework, so I was sure she'd say 'yes'.

"**Absolutely not,**" said Mistress Ring, picking up the potion box. "**My potions are unspeakably dangerous … if you drink them without a teacher. They belong in the incredible, impenetrable teachers' store cupboard in the Teachers' Wing. Far away from students.**"

I'd seen the Teachers' Wing, but I'd never been inside (it's against the rules, obviously).

An idea danced around the corners of my brain.

Maybe I could get that vanishing potion after all.

Just as soon as everyone was asleep.

*

The rest of the day moved even more slowly than me in stomping boots.

But eventually I was in bed, staring at the shape of Walloping's bottom pushing through the bunk above mine.

I knew everyone else was asleep because the dorm sounded like this:

SNURRRGLE.

BURP!

FLOOOOGLEFUFFLEMMMM.

BLARGHHHHUUUURP.

PARP!

So, no one heard me swing my stilts out of bed.

No one heard me clatter between the bunk beds in the dark.

No one heard me ever so slowly turn the big round dormitory door handle.

And when I only opened it a fraction, they didn't wake up as a crack of light crawled through the room.

No one knew I was gone.

Well, no one apart from Kevin, the school slug. But even scary, eye-tentacle-waving, mouth-gnashing giant slugs can't talk. So, I thought I'd be okay.

Outside, the wind whipped around my ears, blowing out every candle on the castle wall with a *whoosh!*

It was cold. And dark. Really dark. I kept one hand on the castle's crumbling, slimy walls and edged towards the Teachers' Wing. If the main school building was like a mountain, the Teachers' Wing was a volcano. Big. Dangerous. And likely to blast me with lava (or Madame Bogbrush's meat-pounding high heels) if anyone caught me.

You might wonder why I was so sure I could break in and steal Mistress Ring's vanishing potion.

That's because you haven't seen the front door. It's big (obviously). But it's made of thick iron bars, just like a prison. If you're a giant, with a giant body and giant hands, you'll *never* be able to squeeze through a door like that.

But me? I put my Small arm and Small hand straight between the bars and, *click*. I opened the lock!

There's a second door behind the bars. I'd seen the teachers come in and out – it's never locked. So, all I had to do was push my whole body against it until,

"*Woah!*"

It swung open.

I blinked in the light of the candles. The Teachers' Wing looked *nothing* like our dormitories. It didn't have a cold stone floor, it had thick red velvet carpets (perfect for sneaking on). The corridor was lined with big gold pots filled with swamp reeds that reached the ceiling. And it didn't smell like bog juice or mould muffins or anything that comes from the swamp. It smelled sweet and comforting, like hot chocolate.

Hang on. It *was* hot chocolate! I followed the delicious smell down the corridor as I looked for the teachers' store cupboard.

"**GOOD DRINKING, TEACHERS,**" boomed Madame Bogbrush's voice from behind a gleaming gold door.

Uh oh.

The teachers weren't asleep yet.

"**Good drinking!**" came the voices of Master Massive, Mr Rather-Large, Miss Sizeable, Mr Ogg, Mistress Ring and Mrs Mahoosive.

I hovered outside the door.

"**HAVE WE GOT THE WHIPPED CREAM?**"

"**Here, Headmistress.**"

"**AND THE TOFFEE SAUCE?**"

"**Here, Headmistress.**"

"**AND THE CHOCOLATE SPRINKLES?**"

"**Here, Headmistress.**"

"**AND THE MARSHMALLOWS?**"

Silence.

"**WHO'S GOT THE MARSHMALLOWS?**"

"**Sorry, Madame Bogbrush,**" said a deep voice.

"**Don't worry, Master Massive. I'll get some more!**" said Mrs Mahoosive. My mouth watered at the thought of hot chocolate, whipped cream, toffee sauce, chocolate sprinkles and marshmallows. I couldn't believe the teachers made us drink boiled bog broth at bedtime when they had hot chocolate. How unfair!

Then my stomach dropped. *Where* was Mrs Mahoosive getting the marshmallows from?

BANG!

The golden door swung open. With *me* hiding behind it.

Chapter fifteen

A Few Marshmallows for Bed

I held my breath and crossed my fingers and toes. I hoped Mrs Mahoosive wouldn't notice my feet, marching behind the staffroom door.

The teacher stomped down the corridor and around the corner. I marched a few steps behind, wobbling between big gold pots of swamp reeds.

Mrs Mahoosive stopped in front of a smaller door than the rest. Small for a giant, that is (it was as big as any normal Small door). A sign above it said, *'TEACHERS' STORE CUPBOARD.'*

I'd found it!

Mrs Mahoosive squeezed inside the cupboard,

with her purple flowery bottom still sticking out the door. A moment later, she pulled out a *whole sack* full of marshmallows.

My stomach groaned longingly.

"Who's there?" said the teacher. **"Ogg, is that you my love? Come out here and give me a kiss!"**

Were Mr Ogg and Mrs Mahoosive in love?! Yuck! I pushed my hand over my growling stomach.

"Strange," said Mrs Mahoosive, shaking her head and trudging away.

Phew.

When everything was quiet, I made a wobbly dash for the store cupboard. The chocolatey smell hit me straight away. I took a long, deep breath. The cupboard was as big as our old living room. But it was even darker than the courtyard. I left the door ajar to help me see.

And there it was! In between boxes marked *Bashing Glove repair kit* and trays labelled *Grunting*

Handkerchiefs was the box of vanishing potions Mistress Ring showed us in class. Five glass bottles with creepy skull-shaped stoppers twinkled at me.

I'm Harvey Small, not Harvey Stealer.

But if I didn't vanish, I'd never find the fortune teller.

If I didn't find the fortune teller, I wouldn't know how to stop myself stealing a giant.

And since giant-stealing grave danger was bound to ruin the show, if I didn't vanish, we'd fail the school inspection, too.

Then the school would close, I'd lose my best friend and the Unspeakable Circus would steal us in the night.

That was all *far* worse than stealing a little vanishing potion. I popped a bottle in my pocket.

CLICKETY.

Uh oh.

CLACKETY.

I'd been too slow.

CLACK.

Madame Bogbrush wasn't in the staffroom anymore.

"**Madame Bogbrush, Madame Bogbrush!**" said Mrs Mahoosive. She was on the move again, too. "**Headmistress, please reconsider this vanishing spell. I know you want to impress the school inspector. But** we can't give students vanishing potion. What would the parents say?"

"THEY'LL THANK ME FOR KEEPING OUR SCHOOL OPEN WITH AN EXCELLENT PERFORMANCE. THEY'LL SAY VANISHING WAS THE BEST SPELL THEY'VE EVER SEEN," said the Headteacher.

I felt a pang of guilt. I hoped Mistress Ring had enough potion left for her finale.

"GOOD SLEEPING, TEACHERS," boomed Madame Bogbrush.

"Good sleeping, Headmistress," said Master Massive, Mr Ogg, Mr Rather-Large, Miss Sizeable, Mistress Ring and Mrs Mahoosive.

At last. If the teachers were going to bed, sneaking back out the cupboard would be easy.

Except…

Through the crack in the door, I could just make out the curve of a giant red shoe. Madame Bogbrush was right outside!

I backed into the corner and pulled a sack of marshmallows in front of me.

"MARGO, YOU LEFT THE DOOR OPEN,

AGAIN," said the Headteacher. The door handle twisted.

I bit my lip to stop myself whimpering.

Light flooded into the cupboard.

And Madame Bogbrush's humungous hand stretched towards me.

It was almost as big as my whole body (without the stilts).

"I'LL JUST TAKE A FEW MARSHMALLOWS FOR BED," she said.

Her hand groped around the cupboard, coming millimetres away from my face!

My heart thudded harder than a giant's tap-dancing stomping boot.

I pushed the sack of marshmallows towards her long gnarly fingers.

The fingers closed around the sweets and slowly backed away.

I didn't dare breathe.

Then... *Click*.

Madame Bogbrush shut the door.

I stood, shaking, in total darkness.

That was close.

When I was sure the teachers had absolutely, definitely gone, I tried to find my way out of the dark, dark cupboard. But I couldn't move.

My right stilt was stuck in something.

I bent down to free it and I felt … a handle.

On the ground.

Inside the cupboard.

A door handle!

Could it be … the Fortune Teller in the Cellar's cellar door handle?

I pulled it open and the cupboard glowed with candlelight. Heavy stone steps twisted underground.

I followed them down, into a cobweb-filled cellar.

It was so chilly down here my breath came out in white swirls. The air was thick with the strangest smell of roses and lavender bags. It reminded me of Great Granny Small's bedroom.

I paused at the bottom step.

This was it.

The moment I'd find out for sure if I'm the Unchosen One. The moment I'd find out how to save the school.

I took a deep breath and prepared to face the Fortune Teller in the Cellar.

Until now, I hadn't imagined what she'd look like.

When I clapped eyes on her, my skin went cold.

She was leaning forward in a wooden rocking chair, hunched over a crystal ball. But I recognised her instantly.

"M-Mum?" I blurted. "What are you doing here?"

Chapter sixteen

Knowing Spoils All the Fun

That's right. My *mum* was sitting in a dark cellar, full of cobwebs and candles. Sitting in the exact spot where the fortune teller should be. It didn't make sense.

"Mum?" I said again. The wobble in my voice was even stronger than the wobble on my stilts.

"I'm not your mother," she said.

Well, that was just charming. Mum dumps me in giant school for a few weeks and forgets about me completely!

"Mum, please! It's me, Harvey," I said. "I'm wearing stilts," I added. Could my own mum really have forgotten me so quickly?

"I know who you are, Harvey Small. I'm not who you think I am."

"Mum, what are you talking about?" I almost yelled. She hadn't given me a hug or anything.

"I am the Fortune Teller in the Cellar."

"I know, Mum, you could have told me," I said. I'd have paid loads more attention when Mum talked about programming her *watchamablasters* and installing *digidoodahs* if I'd known she was secretly predicting the future.

"I'm not your mother," she said again. She stood up, placing her hands on the wooden table in front of her. She didn't move like Mum. She was slow and creaky like that old rocking chair she'd been sitting in.

"I am as old as time and as young as the stars," she croaked. "I am the wind through the trees and the beat of your heart. I am the Fortune Teller in the Cellar. I see the start of everything. I know the start of everything. And my predictions always come true," she said.

Hmm. She sounded and looked less like Mum by the second.

"Smalls find my predictions hard to hear, for I only speak the truth," Possibly-Not-My-Mum continued.

"It's why I appear as someone you trust. A boy must listen to his mother. So, you shall listen to me. I have an important prediction."

She looked fierce now. I felt my head nodding all by itself.

"*GRAVE DANGER ... will come from one who's not who they say. An innocent giant will be stolen away. Beware the Unchosen One,*" she said.

Then she slumped into the chair, closed her eyes and rocked forwards and back over the crystal ball.

Had I, somehow, completely accidentally ... killed her? Whoever she was. My stomach lurched. This was like Rodney Hamster all over again. I gave the fortune teller a prod.

Her chest heaved up and down.

She wasn't dead, she was asleep!

"Wake up!" I said. "I need to know what happens next."

Silence.

Not a whisper.

Only a gentle snore.

I stood there, staring at the fortune teller by the light of the candles. After all the effort I'd made to find her, she couldn't just go to sleep.

"Answer me!" I cried.

The fortune teller sat bolt upright and smiled. "Sorry, I must have nodded off. Predicting things is very tiring," she said.

Relief washed over me. This time, I'd get answers.

"That's okay," I said, rubbing my hands together to keep warm. "I need to know if I'm the Unchosen One. If I am, how can I save the school?"

"*GRAVE DANGER…*" she started up again.

"No!" I said, jumping in to stop her. "I've heard that bit. What happens next?"

She stared into her crystal ball, said, "Ooooh," and wiggled her fingers.

I held my breath.

Finally, *finally* I'd get an answer.

The fortune teller sighed and slumped into her rocking chair. "Absolutely no idea," she said.

"What?" I shook my head. Was my future so terrible she didn't want to tell me?

"I do the beginning of predictions," she said. "My twin sister does the end."

I peered behind her into the gloom of the cellar. "Okay, where's your sister?"

"In Small City. Making predictions. Mostly for

herself. She wins the lottery a lot. Smalls like her, as long as she shares her winnings with them. They don't like me. Everyone wants to know how the story ends. They're less bothered about the start. Don't know why. I think knowing spoils all the fun."

I blinked back unexpected tears.

"So, you don't know *anything* that can help me?" I said, feeling hope fizzle away.

"I don't need to," she said. "You already have the answers."

"I do?" This was baffling. Why would I spend weeks searching for the fortune teller if I had the answers?

"In your pocket," she said, with a knowing look. My hand closed round the bottle of stolen vanishing potion. My cheeks flushed.

"I'm sorry, I didn't mean to take it. I'll put it back," I blurted. My voice trembled.

The fortune teller shrugged. "No, you won't," she said, staring into her crystal ball again.

Okay, she *definitely* wasn't Mum. If Mum knew I'd been stealing, I'd never hear the end of it. She'd march me straight up to Mistress Ring to say 'sorry.'

The fortune teller frowned.

"I do have another prediction for you," she said. There was a twinkle in her eye.

Okay, *now* I'd get some proper help.

"*Look before you leap*," she croaked. Then she fell back into her rocking chair and started snoring again.

Look before you leap? That's not even a prediction. It's just a saying. Which is exactly what I'd have told the fortune teller if she'd had the decency to be awake.

"Hello?" I said, shaking her arm, "HELLO?"

It was no good. She was fast asleep.

I wobbled back up the stone cellar steps. My eyes blurred with disappointed tears.

But it didn't matter.

I still had Mistress Ring's vanishing potion in my pocket.

If the potion somehow held the answers, it was time to use it.

Chapter seventeen

Orange

Maybe I should have spotted a few clues that drinking vanishing potion was a bad idea. You know, little things like:

- it's got a creepy skull on the bottle
- it's such a bright shade of blue it actually *glows*
- it was deliberately locked in a cupboard to keep it AWAY from young giants (and Smalls).

But this was a school-saving emergency. And the

fortune teller had practically told me to drink it, hadn't she?

I freed Lord Pawington Bear-Face Grumple Snout the Second from the underpants I'd hidden him in. Vanishing would almost certainly be fine if I had my favourite teddy with me for protection.

With Mr Snout safely under my arm, I pulled the skull-shaped stopper off Mistress Ring's vanishing potion. The thick blue liquid smelled of disinfectant and sweaty cheese. (Another sign it might not be the best idea to drink it. But I was used to swamp food now. *Everything* here smelled like feet. Even the puddings.)

I looked over to Walloping. My best friend drooled as he slept. A wide grin filled his snoring face. I wished he could vanish with me, but I didn't think I'd have enough potion for both of us. I'd be safer with my old best friend instead.

"Okay Mr Snout, here we go," I whispered.

I drank down the potion in a single gulp.

My hands shook, my head swam, my skin prickled and burned.

I dropped the bottle with a *smash!*

Then everything went orange.

Chapter eighteen

A Warning Sign

When I opened my eyes, I expected to be invisible.

Instead, I was lying in a pile of Walloping's dirty old socks that he'd dumped by the side of our bunk beds. And Norma Enormous, Gallumphing Doorknob and Walloping were all looking at me. Their faces were shaped like worry and shiny with dribble. A tear dripped down Walloping's cheek and splashed me in the face.

"Oh boy, oh boy, oh boy, you is alive!" he said, pulling me into a hug so tight it squeezed all the air from my chest.

My head ached. My throat was dry. I hadn't

disappeared. And nope, I wasn't any closer to saving the school from grave danger. At least, I didn't think I was.

"The Unchosen One tries to steal one of us in the night!" said Walloping, still squeezing me tight.

I wriggled free and sat up. Maybe the fortune teller was right. Maybe the vanishing potion *did* have the answers.

"But you scares them off when you started singing," said Gallumphing, shaking the side of the bunk bed and stomping his feet.

Singing?

Oh no. That's why I felt so rotten.

I hadn't been singing.

I'd been *sick*. (It explained why I smelled worse than a rotting pond weed smoothie, too.)

Was that why I didn't vanish?

"How do you know the Unchosen One was here?" I asked. My head was groggy, but my insides fluttered with hope. Maybe I wasn't the Unchosen One. Maybe someone else really did try and steal a giant.

"They l-l-leaves this," said Walloping.

You'll never believe it, but Walloping was holding Lord Pawington Bear-Face Grumple Snout the Second by the ear. He dropped my teddy on the floor like it was made of snot and fire.

The giants gasped.

A few covered their eyes.

Lumbering whimpered.

And all my hope fluttered away.

I winced as Norma Enormous snatched Mr Snout by the head. "It's not dangerous *now*," she said.

My bear's right button-eye clattered onto the floor.

I reached up to rescue the rest of him, but Norma pulled Mr Snout away. Bits of stuffing fell out of his paws.

"The Unchosen One is obviously a Small," said Norma. "They left this teddy as a warning sign."

She dropped Mr Snout face-down on the floor.

I scooped him up and instinctively stroked his squashed, one-eyed head.

Gallumphing, Norma and Walloping stared at me. Their mouths hung open.

Oops.

I scrunched my face into the same horrified frown as everyone else. I'd give Mr Snout a proper hug when they weren't around.

"I can ask the teachers to call my Ma if you like?" said Norma. "She's the best doctor this side of the Moaning Marsh. The shock could have given you Gurgling Brainbox. It's pretty serious."

"Gurgling Brainbox?" I repeated. I'd never heard of it.

"Yeah, she'll send a medical worm up your nose to have a quick look around. If it comes out your ear, you're fine. If it doesn't ... well, it's best not to think about that." Norma's face turned a worrying shade of green.

"No! I don't need any doctors!" I blurted. I didn't want anything up my nose or in my ear thank you very much. And I definitely didn't want doctors prodding around my stilts.

"Suit yourself," said Norma. "I've told Mistress Ring

what happened, anyway. She's my favourite teacher, so I know she'll save us from the Unchosen One."

I gulped.

Seeing Mistress Ring might be even worse than seeing a swamp doctor. What if she knew I'd stolen her vanishing potion?

Norma kept talking, "Oh, and Mistress Ring gave me the vanishing slot in the grand finale. She told me this morning. Apparently, I'm the *only* giant who can juggle seven flaming clubs and cartwheel at the same time. Backwards. Wearing a blindfold," Norma said, puffing out her chest.

Poor Norma. She looked so pleased with herself. Should I tell her the vanishing potion didn't work?

I didn't have time to decide.

Mistress Ring had already arrived.

"**Roll up, roll up to breakfast,**" she said to my friends, "**I'll take *good care* of Harvey.**"

Walloping hesitated. Then his stomach *roarrrred.* "I'll saves you a mould muffin!" he said, before bounding out the door.

I sat on my bunk and gave Mistress Ring my most innocent, I-really-am-very-poorly smile.

The teacher smoothed out the edges of her long

red jacket and marched on the spot. I still thought it was odd that she walked like me.

"I hope you get well soon," she said. Her icy smile made me shiver more than the fortune teller's cellar. "I'd hate anything *unspeakable* to happen in your sleep," she added.

"Er, thank you?" I said. Giants had a funny way of making each other feel better.

"Dangerous things are happening in this school," she said, marching over to the dorm window. "Terrifying, horrifying, *unspeakable* things."

I wasn't going to argue. I knew I was the terrifying, horrifying thing she was talking about.

"*Someone* stole one of my Extra Special Top-Secret Vanishing Potions last night. Can you believe it?" she said. "I don't know what the inspector will say when she sees Madame Bogbrush is running a school for thieves."

My stomach twisted itself into a hundred knots. Could the school be shut down because of me?

"If I find out who did it," she said, turning around and prodding me in the chest, "I'm going to do something dreadful to them. Something so terrible that I can't even name it. Something too hideous to talk about. Something … *unspeakable,*" she said.

Then she stalked out the room. I gave my bedraggled teddy a squeeze.

I was confused.

If Mistress Ring knew what I was up to, why hadn't she stomped on me?

*

Mrs Mahoosive didn't send me to a swamp doctor (phew!). But she said I could spend the whole day in bed to recover from my *brush with the Unchosen One.* That meant a day when I couldn't dance badly or upset the school inspector or bring any danger to the school whatsoever.

Or so I thought.

At bedtime, Walloping charged into the dorm first. "Best friend, best friend, we's had a brilliant idea!" he said, bounding between the bunk beds.

Norma raced after him. "The teachers are all busy worrying about the inspection," she said. "Now we know the Unchosen One wants to steal a truly gifted giant, we must protect ourselves." She put her hands on her hips. "To stop the Unchosen One getting in

140

again and spoiling my grand vanishing finale, we're going to take turns guarding the school gate. Starting tonight."

"But Madame Bogbrush will stomp you into a sandwich!" I cried. "It's rule 32." If my friends got caught sneaking around at night, they'd get into BIG trouble. And it would all be my fault.

Norma scratched her head. "You're right ... I probably shouldn't go first," she said. "I'm the star of our show after all."

I knew what I had to do.

"I'll guard the gate," I said. (Since I was only guarding it from *me*, how hard could it be?)

"Oh boy, oh boy, oh boy!" said Walloping. "I's been practising my sneaking. I'll guard with you."

And my heart sank. Walloping was my best friend in the whole world. But sneaking out at night with the loudest, clumsiest giant in school was almost certainly a terrible idea.

Chapter nineteen

Things That Go
Rurrooooghhhh in the Night

Walloping really had practised his sneaking. And somehow, on the first night of our gate-guarding duty, he made it out the dorm and across the field without making a peep.

I was about to tell him how brilliant I thought he was when…

Creeeeaaaaaak.

The great golden gate at the back of the field opened.

We stopped where we were, in the middle of the long grass.

"Oh no, oh no, oh no!" whispered Walloping. "Teachers is the only ones with keys to the gate. Maybe someone hears me after all."

"Quick, hide in the tall trees!" I said, hurrying to the edge of the field. If a teacher *was* out here and we charged across the courtyard, they'd hear us stomping on the cobbles.

A strange sound echoed across the field.

It was a rattling, rumbling, trumpeting *Rurroooghhh!* More animal than human. It was even louder than a giant's snore.

Rurrooooghhhh!

"I doesn't likes it out here!" yelped Walloping, pulling his hands over his ears. "The Unchosen One is going to get us!" His eyes were wide with fear.

I was scared too. But at least I was sure I was the Unchosen One. Nothing in the school could be more dangerous than me.

I *had* to see what was making that noise.

I edged towards the gate.

"Don't leaves me!" whispered Walloping.

I stayed close to the trees, keeping my head down and sticking to the shadows.

Walloping tiptoed behind me, whimpering all the way.

Then we saw it.

Just outside the gate.

Two white tusks that glistened in the moonlight. And a white, bony frame ... surrounded by a hazy grey shadow. With flapping shadow ears. And the wisp of a long, curling trunk.

"It's a ... a ... a *skelephant*!" blurted Walloping. "I has seen them in my *Big Book for Explorers*! They was elephants once." He shuddered, "Now they is dead and alive *at the same time*. They is not from the swamp, they is from ... the world!"

"Wh-wh-what's an elephant, I mean skelephant, doing in the middle of the swamp?" I whispered. The creature looked terrifying, like a walking X-ray picture. But Walloping didn't seem scared at all.

Something clanked around the skelephant's bony feet. Someone had chained it to a tree outside the school gates.

And someone was talking to it.

"**Shut it, Twinkle, you noisy beast,**" said a booming voice I'd heard before.

"*Rurroooooghhhh!*" said the skelephant.

Crack!

In the moonlight, I could just make out the curve of a whip, dancing through the air. It hit the ground next to the skelephant's chained foot.

The skelephant stopped trumpeting.

"Tomorrow, the most gifted giant will be ours. Our unspeakably unspeakable show will be even more unspeakable. Now, stay quiet."

Most gifted giant?

Unspeakably unspeakable show?

I turned back to Walloping. "Walloping, do you know who that is?" I said.

He stared blankly at me. "Ummm, a skelephant trainer?"

I shook my head.

"It's Mistress Ring!"

Even in the darkness, I could see flashes of Walloping's wonky grin.

"Oh boy, oh boy, oh boy!" he said, jumping from foot to foot, kicking up leaves. "If Mistress Ring has a skelephant do you thinks she'll lets me play with it? I has always wanted to play with creatures from the world. Even the undead ones."

"Shhh!" I said. My best friend's whispers were turning into shouts.

"**What in the Blazing Big Top was that?**" said Mistress Ring, turning to face us in the dark. I pushed my small hands over Walloping's large, dribbly mouth.

The skelephant grunted. I watched as this strange creature somehow picked up a football-sized ball with its shadowy trunk. The ball's shiny white leather caught the moonlight. I couldn't remember the last time I'd played. I missed it.

Mistress Ring shrugged. **"You're right, Twinkle. It's probably swamp goblins. The giants will be snoring for hours, yet,"** she said. **"Still, you'd better hide again."** She threw a huge swamp-coloured cloak over the skelephant.

"Back! Back!" she said, cracking her whip at the skelephant's bony feet until it edged into the swamp trees.

"Tomorrow, as soon as we wakes up, I is going to play with that skelephant!" whispered Walloping.

"No, Walloping, you can't!" I said.

Something was wrong. Very wrong.

The way everyone said Mistress Ring was a Country Giant like me, even though I'd made Country Giants up.

The way her vanishing potion didn't make me vanish.

The way she talked about all the *unspeakable* things she'd do to the person who stole the potion.

The skelephant she'd hidden in the swamp.

"What's wrong? Why can't I plays with the skelephant?" said Walloping.

I said, "Because if you do, the teacher will know you were out of bed."

"Awww, fiddle clubs!" said Walloping, hanging his head.

But that wasn't the real reason.

I'd finally figured it out.

I didn't think Mistress Ring was a teacher at all.

She was someone much more *unspeakable* than that.

Chapter twenty

The Dress Rehearsal

My brain and my stomach felt like they were bursting with fireworks. Mistress Ring wasn't who she said she was (and I *didn't* think she wanted to teach us spelling). If I was right, it meant I wasn't dangerous! Well, not giant-stealingly dangerous, anyway.

The next morning, Walloping thrust his *Big Book for Explorers* at me. He'd opened it on the Skelephant page.

"Are you thinking what I'm thinking?" I said.

"Are you thinking you is hungry and ready for breakfast?" said Walloping.

The Skelephant

Both dead and alive at the same time, this mostly gentle creature was once a living elephant. It has a recognisable grey shadow surrounding its bony body – a memory of its original shape. The skelephant's shadow is see-through, but strong. It can still use its trunk and ears.

Like many animals, elephants were tricked into joining the Unspeakable Circus by an evil Ring Mistress hundreds of years ago.

Upon joining the circus, the elephants were bound by a Never-Ending Contract. It forced them to perform in this life. And the next. The show, as the Unspeakable Circus says, must always go on.

"No!" I cried. How could my gifted best friend not see? His book made everything so clear.

"I think Mistress Ring might be the ... Unchosen One," I whispered. "I think she's the evil Ring Mistress from the Unspeakable Circus. And she's brought the skelephant with her."

Just saying it out loud made me feel a weird mix of worry and relief. The school's troubles really weren't my fault.

Then I thought about today's dress rehearsal, and

the unspeakable truth hit me. "I think Mistress Ring wants to steal Norma Enormous."

Walloping shook his head. "Oh, best friend, you is so funny. Norma can't be in danger from a teacher. They is rubbish at guarding the gate, but teachers are still here to look after us. Mistress Ring probably rescues the skelephant from the Unspeakable Circus." He shook his head again and bounded off to breakfast.

It didn't matter. Whether Walloping believed me or not, I knew one thing. I had to stop Norma from vanishing.

*

Everyone was talking about the dress rehearsal at breakfast.

"My dad will be so impressed when he sees the way I dance the cancan tomorrow!" said Gallumphing Doorknob, snapping his Lycra leotard straps. "He's taken a day off clout coaching just to watch me. *And* he said he's going to bring some of the giants from Clouters United to cheer us on!"

The giants stomped and cheered at the thought of meeting the stars from their dorm room posters.

"Well, my ma will never believe it when she sees

how long I can twirl on one leg without falling over!" said Jumbolina. (It was about half a second – the class record.)

"It's going to be the best performance ever!" said Maxi and Maximus Maximus together.

I wasn't so sure. I really wanted to dance well for Mum and Dad. I still hoped that if I danced brilliantly, they might be so happy that they'd stop fighting and we could all live together again. But Mistress Ring (or should I say, the evil Ring Mistress) was clearly up to something. And Norma Enormous needed to know about it.

I found Norma eating a pile of swamp snails at the back of the dining hall. She'd decorated her hair with empty snail shells. And her leotard was sparklier than the slime trails Kevin

the school slug left in the corridors. I squinted to look at her.

"I need energy for my big finale," she said. "Doing a vanishing spell is probably hungry work."

I tried not to wince as Norma squelched her fingernail inside an oversized shell. She pulled out a snail the size of a sausage. I longed for a nice, boring bowl of cereal.

"Norma," I said. "I don't think you should drink vanishing potion in the dress rehearsal."

Norma shook her head. "I should have known you'd be jealous," she said. "You want the finale spot for yourself."

I sighed. Norma's so competitive. I should have known she'd say I'd be jealous.

"No, Norma, it's not that," I said. I had to explain.

"**There she is. The finest! The most grotesque, I mean the *greatest*! The one, the only, Norma Enormous!**" said the evil Ring Mistress, marching towards us. "**I hope you're not bothering our star performer,**" said the unspeakable teacher. She flashed me a steely glare before reaching her arm around Norma. "**Luckily no one has stolen any more Extra Special Top-Secret Vanishing Potions, so we have** plenty left for you. I just need you to sign a little contract for me. Something to say you're happy to be the star of the show. Come with me."

"Norma! Wait!" I cried. The Ring Mistress was going to get Norma to sign a Never-Ending Contract. If she signed it, she'd belong to the circus. Forever!

Norma didn't look back.

DING!

DING!

DING!

The ear-numbing, bone-shaking showtime bells were ringing. It was too late.

I followed the others to the stage Mr Ogg had built for us. It teetered in the middle of the stomping ground behind the castle.

"**Places please!**" yelled Mrs Mahoosive.

Mr Ogg blasted ballet tunes on his trumpet.

Madame Bogbrush tapped her meat-pounding shoes to the music.

Ms Sugar Plum tutted.

Mrs Mahoosive roared instructions at us.

"**Chins up everybody!**"

"**Shoulders back, Biggus Biggins!**"

"Stop picking your nose, Gina Gigantic!"

"Beautiful, Blundering Teapot!"

It was deafening.

I couldn't see the Ring Mistress anywhere. And I had to be on stage.

Our maypole dancing was dreadful.

"Help, the dancing stick is eating me!" moaned Lumbering, tying himself up in the maypole ribbons. Walloping, Gallumphing and I dragged him off stage.

The twins flung each other around in a pretty good disco dancing duet. Good until Maxi got carried away and threw Maximus Maximus off the stage completely and onto Mr Ogg's head.

Soon all we had left (thank goodness) was the final class cancan. And Norma's vanishing spell.

Except I was certain she wouldn't vanish.

Norma paced behind us. "You'd better dance brilliantly!" she said. "I don't want anyone messing up my big moment."

"Norma, please," I said, trying one last time to warn her. "Don't drink the potion!"

"I'm not listening!" she said, sticking her fingers in her ears.

Mr Ogg's trumpet trumpeted the cancan tune.

It was time.

We cancanned onto the stage.

The floorboards sagged in the middle.

I looked back to Norma. She was holding a bottle of vanishing potion. "Norma, I'm not jealous. I promise!" I said.

She shook her head, uncorked the potion and took a great big gulp.

What could I do? Madame Bogbrush and the school inspector were watching. I held my head up, plastered a fake grin on my face and danced.

Kick up and left. Smile.

Kick up and right. Shoulders back.

Kick up and left. Smile.

We all kicked and grinned like lunatics. The stage bent and wobbled under our giant dancing feet.

Mr Ogg played faster. And faster. And faster.

All I could hear was the *Toot!* of the trumpet. The *Bang!* of our feet. The *TAPTAPTAP* of Madame Bogbrush's shoes. And Mrs Mahoosive yelling **"FASTER! HIGHER! KICK GIANTS, KICK!"**

For one frantic, leg-kicking moment, I think we were almost *good*.

In that blur of shouting and music and dancing, our cancan line parted.

Norma Enormous danced forwards. She kicked higher and faster than all of us.

Then she started swaying.

The stage *creaked* and *groaned*.

Out of the corner of my eye, I saw the flash of a red jacket in the wings.

Mistress Ring threw something small and round at the front of the stage.

It burst with a *BANG!*

The stage filled with smoke.

I couldn't see!

We stopped kicking.

"Arghh!"

"Oww!"

"Oof!"

We started crashing into each other instead.

When the smoke cleared, we coughed, spluttered and counted our bruises.

All of us apart from one.

Norma Enormous had vanished.

How would you rate the school's overall performance?

Utter chaos.

They seem to have made a student disappear, though. Impressive magic, but not the kind of spell the Beastly School Board is looking for.

Recommendations:

Giants should not wear sludge-brown tutus with sludge-brown leotards. They're so last season. I suggest trying something pink. With a tiara.

Keep an eye on the sneaking, whispering boy with the small hands, wobbly walk, bloody nose and three-headed worm who wants to vanish. He stood completely still during tap dancing. Why?

158

Chapter twenty-one

Follow That Skelephant!

The dress rehearsal was over. The smoke from the grand finale had cleared. And through our coughing, I heard a noise. It started as a low rumble and got louder and louder.

"*BRAVO! BRAVO!*"

The *whole* school was cheering. Even the teachers. Even Ms Sugar Plum! Norma Enormous had vanished, just like Mistress Ring (the evil Ring Mistress) said she would.

"What's wrong, Harvey? Why isn't you cheering?" said Walloping, thumping his hands together.

"Still jealous of Norma's spell?" said Jumbolina.

"No!" I said. I wished everyone would stop calling me jealous. "I think Norma should come back now. It's only a good vanishing spell if someone vanishes *and* reappears."

My classmates scratched their heads.

"You is right," said Walloping. "She is only meant to be gones for five minutes. How many more minutes is that?"

The giants shrugged. In all the smoke, no one had looked at a watch. But I was sure Norma wasn't coming back.

"Walloping," I whispered, "I really think we should..." I began.

"Shh!" said Walloping. Like the others, he was waiting to cheer Norma's return. His eyes were wide and his smile was even wider.

"Walloping!" I said again, tugging on his leotard strap. The longer we waited, the longer we were giving the Ring Mistress to escape with Norma.

"Shh! She'll be heres any minute!" he said, brushing me away. Then he went back to clasping his hands and jiggling on his toes.

Gradually though, those giant smiles fell into frowns.

160

The whispers became worried.

Until Walloping, who looked like he might explode if he had to wait one second longer yelled, "Norma! You cans come back now!"

The others shouted too and peered around the back of the stage.

Of course, there was no sign of Norma. Or the Ring Mistress.

Ms Sugar Plum tutted again.

"**NORMA ENORMOUS, REAPPEAR RIGHT NOW!**" bellowed Madame Bogbrush,

The stage wobbled and shook behind us.

But Norma didn't reappear.

The penny finally dropped.

"The Unchosen One has stolen Norma!" said Lumbering, flinging himself onto the ground in despair.

I pulled Walloping away from the others.

"Now do you believe me?" I whispered, sticking my head in his wide, waxy ear. "Mistress Ring's taken Norma. I'm telling you, *she's* the Unchosen One!"

"**I WILL NOT ALLOW OUR BEST STUDENT TO BE STOLEN!**" said Madame Bogbrush. The Headteacher stamped her meat-pounding feet.

And the whole stage collapsed.

"Arrghhhhhhhhh!" cried everyone at once, dodging flying strips of wood, velvet curtain and Ms Sugar Plum's clipboard.

Ms Sugar Plum tutted. "Amateurs!" she scoffed.

Walloping's face crumpled with worry. I knew what I had to do.

"Walloping, you want to see the world, don't you?" I asked.

"You knows I do," said Walloping. His bottom lip wobbled.

"Then follow me. We're going to rescue Norma and prove to Ms Sugar Plum that we're saving the school!"

Walloping hesitated. He looked over to the teachers – they were searching for Norma in the ruins of the stage. I knew she wasn't there.

"Walloping, come on! I need you to show me the way through the swamp. You've got all the maps!" I said.

Walloping fiddled with his sock elastic.

Even when Walloping was squeezed into his Lycra dancing dungarees and tutu, he carried rolled-up maps in his socks.

"Pleeeeeaaaaaassssssssssssse help me search the swamp? For Norma? To be an explorer?" I said.

Walloping gave me a dribbly grin and yanked out a crumpled (and slightly sweaty) map of the swamp. "Okay!"

We ran as fast as my stilts could carry me, across the long grass and towards the great golden gate.

It was wide open.

And there they were.

Norma Enormous.

Twinkle the skelephant.

And the evil Ring Mistress.

We raced through the field towards them.

"Norma! Comes back!" yelled Walloping.

Norma's eyes were half-closed. She swayed like a blade of the long grass. Of course! The vanishing potion must really be *sleeping* potion. If it was strong enough to send Norma to sleep, I'm not surprised it made me sick.

With one shove from the Ring Mistress, Norma slumped over Twinkle the skelephant's bony back.

Twinkle gave an indignant *"Rurrooooooghhhh!"* and dropped her football in the grass. The skelephant's knees cracked and wobbled under Norma's weight.

The three of them charged into the Stinking, Sinking Swamp.

I tried not to think about the hissing swamp goblin with the yellow eyes. The one I'd seen the last time I was in the swamp.

"Quick! Follow that skelephant!" I yelled.

Walloping stumbled over something as we ran through the gate.

"Who left these sticks here?!" he moaned.

"I don't know, keep running!" I said.

"Faster, Twinkle, faster!" cried the Ring Mistress, forcing her skelephant deeper along the swamp's sludgy dirt tracks.

"*Rurroooooghhhh!*" trumpeted Twinkle. The grey shadow of her tail flicked as she trudged.

Twinkle was large, but she wasn't fast. (You wouldn't be either if you'd been dead for two hundred years and had a giant the size of Norma Enormous on your back.)

"Don't worry, Norma! We'll save you!" I cried. Then coughed. My nose filled with the full force of mouldy swamp stench.

"Oh boy, oh boy, oh boy. The world! I sees the world!" said Walloping.

"**Go back to school, you'll never catch the mighty, magnificent Twinkle!**" yelled the Ring Mistress. She'd have scared me more if she wasn't holding her nose and spluttering.

Norma moaned. Her head swung from side to side like a rag doll. She was fast asleep.

We ran further into the swamp. The drooping trees grew thicker. The ground grew sludgier. The stink grew stinkier.

"You didn't tell me the world was so wet!" said Walloping, splashing through a muddy puddle. He flared his nostrils and gave a gigantic sniff. "But boy does it smell good."

This bit of the world did *not* smell good. It smelled worse than a giant's dancing socks after a whole term of dancing. The further we ran, the worse it got.

I don't think Twinkle liked the pong either. She slowed down. And no matter how much the Ring Mistress screamed at her to hurry, she kept on plodding.

"We're catching them!" I said.

The Ring Mistress shook her head. "**Fine, I'll get off,**" she said, hopping onto the soggy ground with a *splosh*! "**Now move faster you dreadful beast!**"

Walloping screamed.

"Mistress Ring's not a giant! She's a Small!" he wailed.

Walloping was right! All this time the Ring Mistress must have been wearing stilts, too. Those were the sticks Walloping tripped over. That's why she marched like me!

"She … she … she be the Unchosen One!" blurted Walloping. At last, my best friend believed me. "We musts stomp and clomp the stinky, rotten Small!" he said.

"That's what I've been telling you!" I said. I tried to ignore the voice in my head. The one that wondered if my best friend would stomp *me* and clomp *me* if he knew I was a Small too.

I kept running.

"Be careful!" said Walloping, reading his map as he ran. "Smalls don't know our safe paths. You needs to turn left before the Moaning Marsh. They is going the wrong way!"

Twinkle the skelephant *splish splashed* on.

So did the Ring Mistress.

Oh no, oh no, oh woahh woahh woahhhh, moaned

the Moaning Marsh as we ran through even soggier ground.

I sprinted past Walloping. If anyone was going to catch the real Unchosen One, I wanted it to be me.

"Harvey! No! It's the wrong way!" cried Walloping.

Ouchy, ouchy, eee! Stop stepping on me! moaned the Moaning Marsh.

I was getting closer.

The Ring Mistress dashed past Twinkle.

I followed.

"It's not safe!" said Walloping.

I was so close.

"Come backs!" said Walloping.

Go away! moaned the Moaning Marsh.

I bent down, stretching out my arms.

I could almost touch the ends of the Ring Mistress' flapping red coat.

Almost.

Almost.

Just a step further.

I reached some more.

"Noooooo!" said Walloping.

Yessss! moaned the Moaning Marsh.

I caught the Ring Mistress by the arm.

"Gotcha!" I cried!

I'd done it! I'd stopped the Unchosen One. I'd saved the school!

But when I turned to pull the Ring Mistress towards Walloping, I couldn't move.

"Uh oh," I said.

My stilts were stuck.

In the swamp.

In the stinking swamp.

In the Stinking, *Sinking* Swamp.

Chapter twenty-two

That Sinking Feeling

If you ever find yourself slowly sinking to your certain death in a stinking swamp pit, it's very important that you DON'T PANIC!!!

But I didn't know that.

All I knew was that thick green swamp sludge was glooping up my stilts.

I wriggled.

I squirmed.

I pulled at my stilts, trying to heave them out the pit.

They wouldn't budge.

The more I panicked, the deeper I fell.

I was sinking faster than a bowling ball in custard.

The Ring Mistress (who wasn't wearing stilts anymore) was sinking, too. Sludge was already up to her stomach.

"Twinkle, save me, you stupid beast!" she cried, waving her arms at the skelephant.

The skelephant plodded closer. Norma Enormous (who was still fast asleep on the skelephant's back) let out a grunting snore. Twinkle bent her head, pushed her grey shadow trunk into the pit ... then squirted the Ring Mistress in the face with swamp sludge.

I'd have laughed – if I hadn't been utterly convinced I was about to die.

"I'll saves you from the world!" said Walloping, lurching towards me.

"No!" I said. If my best friend got sucked in, it would be all my fault! "Stay where you are!"

Walloping slid to a halt, just missing the pit.

The Ring Mistress clung on to my stilt legs. **"No one sinks the Unspeakable Ring Mistress!"** she said. **"I am Unspeakable *and* Unsinkable! All I need is that gifted giant, and my circus show will be unspeakably perfect."**

Walloping stretched his arm towards me. "Grabs my hand!"

The Ring Mistress pushed me down into the cold, lumpy goo. She reached for Walloping instead.

There was no way out.

I was sinking too fast.

Then a voice rang in my ears. A voice that wasn't coming from the Moaning Marsh.

Look before you leap.

There was one way I could save myself. And the Fortune Teller in the Cellar knew it.

But I risked losing my Small-loathing best friend forever.

"Walloping, you know you're my best friend, right?" I said, as the sludge reached the top of my stilts.

"Of course I knows," said Walloping.

"I'm going to jump. I need you to catch me," I said.

Walloping nodded his head like it was on a spring.

I ripped down my dancing dungarees.

"What is you doing?! I can sees your bottom!" said Walloping, smacking his hand over his mouth.

Spotty blue underpants were the least of my problems. I *had* to unstrap my stilts. My hands were so shaky and thick with mud, it took me three goes. But finally, *click*, *click*. I freed my feet from the stilts.

The Ring Mistress looked at me with wide eyes. **"You're one of us! I knew it! You thieving, lying toe rag of a child,"** she said, lunging for my stilts.

I couldn't fall now.

"I'm jumping, Walloping! 1, 2, 3 … catch me!"

I sprang off my stilts and flew through the air…

The last thing I heard was Walloping scream.

Chapter twenty-three

The Leap

The good news is that when I flew off my stilts, I landed right in the middle of Walloping's thick, hairy arms.

The bad news is that Walloping looked ready to throw me straight back into the sink pit.

"You … you … you … is a…" Walloping began.

I nodded, staring up into my best friend's big watery eyes. "I'm a Small. I'm so sorry. I wish I was a giant like you!"

Walloping's tears splashed over me like salty sea waves.

"B-b-but you is a Country Giant. You is going to

show me the world," he said. Snot bubbled out of his nose.

"You're looking at the world right now!" I said. Would he still be my best friend?

The Ring Mistress cut in. Mud from the sink pit bubbled around her chin.

"**Boys! I'm your teacher. I DEMAND that you save me!**" she said, spitting sludge with every word. She was sinking fast.

Walloping shook his head. "You isn't a real teacher. You belongs with the swamp goblins!" he said, turning his back on her.

"**Nooo!**" shrieked the Ring Mistress. Her bright green eyes were wide and wild as the sink pit pulled her under. "**I am the Great Ring Mistress of the Unspeakable Circus. The show…**"

Blob.

"**…will…**"

Blob.

"**…go…**"

Blob.

"**…on.**"

The Ring Mistress' head sank beneath the surface of the sink pit.

"*Rurooghhh!*" trumpeted Twinkle. Norma Enormous rocked from side to side on the skelephant's back. She was still asleep.

Twinkle raised her shadow trunk. Was it a trick of the swamp light, or was Twinkle's grey shadow *twinkling*?

I felt like I was twinkling all over.

"We've done it!" I said. "We've saved the school from the Unchosen One ... and the Unspeakable Circus!" I hadn't felt this good since the last time I beat my keepie-uppie record.

"Yippee!" said Walloping, flinging his arms (and me) up in air. Luckily, he caught me again.

But one thing still bothered me.

"What did you say about swamp goblins?" I asked. The yellow-eyed creature that jumped on Mr Ogg's van and whispered through our dorm window gave me the creeps.

"I doesn't even needs to read about them in my *Big Book for Explorers*," said Walloping, waving me around like a rag doll. "Everyone knows swamp goblins eats only mud ... and anyone who sinks into the swamp."

I shivered. I wondered if the swamp goblins were eating my extra-long dancing dungarees right now.

"*Rurooghhh*!" Twinkle trumpeted again. I bet she was picturing swamp goblins gobbling up her unspeakable owner.

The skelephant was so loud that…

"Ugh! What's going on? Where am I? Did I vanish? Was I the best? Arghhhh!"

Norma Enormous finally woke up.

"ARGHHHH," said Norma Enormous again.

"ARGHHHHHHH!

ARGHHHHH!

ARGHHH!

ARGH.

ARGHHHHHHHHHHHHHHHHHHHH!"

Walloping put me down carefully and ran over to her.

"Shh, Norma, you is okay!" he said.

Norma Enormous leaped off Twinkle's back. "It's a … a … a…" she gibbered.

"A skelephant, we knows," said Walloping.

Norma pointed a shaky finger at me. "And you … you … you're a…"

"He's a Small, we knows that, too," said Walloping.

"And I can see his…" Norma pointed at my blue underpants.

"His bottom, I knows," said Walloping.

Norma's face turned as green as the swamp. I thought she was going to be sick.

"Harvey saves you from bad Mistress Ring. She tries to steal you for herself. She wants to take you to the Unspeakable Circus on a skelephant. She be the Unchosen One!"

Norma shook her head. "Sizzling swamp sprouts, what rubbish!" said Norma. But she didn't sound as sure as usual. "Harvey's just jealous that *I'm* in the grand vanishing finale and he isn't," said Norma.

"Oh yeah?" said Walloping. "Then why is you in the swamp? And why was you riding a skelephant?"

She frowned. For once, Norma Enormous didn't have an answer.

"Should we stomp on him anyway? Just to be safe? ...It's in the rules," she said, eyeing me up suspiciously.

I couldn't believe it. I'd nearly died trying to save Norma and she wanted to stomp on me!

"No!" said Walloping folding his arms. "Harvey Small might be a Small but he still be my best friend."

"I am?" I said, staring up at Walloping.

Walloping gave me his dribbliest grin yet.

"Of course you is. You shares your food. You makes me laugh. You doesn't think I is silly for wanting to sees the world when all the other giants tells me I can't." Walloping paused. "You is the bestest giant I has ever met. Even if you isn't a giant."

My heart did a thousand and thirty-eight somersaults.

We were best friends, *real* best friends.

Yippeeeeee! said the Moaning Marsh, sounding a lot less moany.

Norma shook her head. "It's not allowed!" she said. "Do you know how many rules you've broken by being out here?" Norma counted them on her fingers. "One, being out past the school gates without a teacher. Two, being out past the school gates without a teacher and not following the safe paths. Three, being out past the school gates without a teacher, not following the safe paths and…"

Walloping's stomach roared.

"…missing lunch."

"The rules isn't broken if you is giant-napped," said Walloping. "There should be new rules if we is saving you."

The swamp bubbled and hissed.

"*I've* not broken rules. I never break rules. I'm the best at following rules," said Norma, straightening the snail shells in her hair. "*You've* broken them."

The swamp spat mud at my knees (and Walloping and Norma's ankles). I wished I was still wearing dungarees.

Even though we'd run a long way from school, Madame Bogbrush's wailing voice echoed on the wind around us, "**NORMA, OH NORMA. WHERE HAS MY MOST GIFTED STUDENT GONE?**"

"We should get back," I said.

The sink pit I'd escaped from bubbled and whirled like a washing machine.

Norma kept counting the rules we'd broken.

"Eight." She pointed at Walloping. "Having an untied shoelace. Nine," she pointed at me. "Being a Small ... Arghhhhh!"

I hoped Norma wouldn't scream *every* time she looked at me from now on.

But Norma wasn't looking at me.

Twinkle trumpeted again.

My mouth fell open. I couldn't believe what I was seeing.

Two small hands rose up, out of the sink pit. Each

hand held a screeching, spitting, cat-sized, green swamp goblin by its pointy ears.

The hands and the goblins were reaching for Norma Enormous.

Chapter twenty-four

There's a Small in the School

The small muddy hands rose higher and higher out of the sink pit. The two green swamp goblins gripped in those hands hissed and spat. They reached for Norma Enormous.

"No!" I cried, leaping in front of Norma. We'd come this far. I wasn't going to let the Ring Mistress steal her now.

"Norma! Walloping! Twinkle! Run!" I said.

Norma and Twinkle ran.

"I isn't leaving you," said Walloping. His voice shook.

"You've got to," I said, sounding braver than I felt. "The Unchosen One wants to steal a giant, not a Small!"

Walloping shook his head. "She wants Norma, not me."

I smiled. This was the scariest thing that had ever happened to me. But even the scariest things aren't quite as scary with a best friend by your side.

The Ring Mistress' head and shoulders rose back up through the sink pit. She was caked in mud and dripping in swamp weed. But her green eyes were clear and piercing. I took a step back and she stretched towards *me*. The swamp goblins wriggled and bit, trying to free themselves from her clenched fists.

I looked around

desperately for something to protect myself with. But there was nothing here apart from mud, mud, mud.

It would have to do.

I bent down, scooping up piles of rotting, stinking sludge and launching them at the Ring Mistress' head. If I covered her eyes with mud, she wouldn't see which way Norma was running. Maybe she'd get lost in the swamp forever.

Walloping copied me, slinging massive mud pies in our old teacher's face.

It wasn't enough.

The Ring Mistress' muddy mouth opened, "**I know who you are, Harvey Small,**" she croaked. "**And something truly *unspeakable* will happen to you for this.**"

I gulped.

But before she could say anything else, there was a gasping, rasping sound. It was like the whole swamp was inhaling.

Then, *Fluuuuuuurrrrrrrrrrrrpppppppppplllllllllgurrrrrgggg leeeeewhoooooooooshhhhhhh.*

Pop!

The Ring Mistress shot up, up, up out of the

swamp. She flew in an arc, higher and higher until she was just a speck in the sky.

I was safe.

Walloping pointed at the sky. "The swamp spits Mistress Ring out! She must taste really bad if even the swamp goblins doesn't eat her."

I tried to picture how much worse the teacher could taste than the bog broth, algae pies and rotten swamp fish stews I'd eaten this term.

We hurried down a winding swamp path after Norma and Twinkle. Norma looked at me with tears in her eyes.

"Y-y-you saved me. You really saved me," she said. "Thank you."

I grinned. Maybe Norma would believe Smalls were good after all.

"Where do you think the Ring Mistress landed?" I asked. It was hard to forget the unspeakable things she wanted to do to me.

"I know, I know, I loves directions," said Walloping. "We're travelling south back to school, and the teacher flew that way," Walloping waved his arm. "So that means she goes east."

Norma cut in. "And looking at how high she flew

and the speed she travelled…" She counted on her fingers. "I'd say she landed right in the middle of the Vampire Mountains. I doubt we'll see her for a long time. If the vampires don't see her first."

I nodded. That sounded far enough away. For now.

But as we trudged back towards the school, I began to feel sick.

After all, I was still a Small. And Smalls weren't allowed in school. Would the giants let me stay?

I didn't have to wait long to find out.

Madame Bogbrush was stomping towards the school gates.

"GREAT GOLIATHS! WHAT'S GOING ON?" boomed the Headteacher. The long grass wilted around her humungous feet.

Ms Sugar Plum and her giant clipboard flew after her.

I gulped. Now I wasn't wearing stilts, Madame Bogbrush looked *even* bigger. I felt like I was standing at the bottom of the world's biggest skyscraper. A skyscraper that was about to stomp on me.

Hiding behind Walloping was no good. The Headteacher's saucer-sized eyes saw everything.

Madame Bogbrush bent low until her head hovered above Walloping, Norma and me.

"NORMA ENORMOUS! IS THAT REALLY YOU?" she asked.

Norma nodded.

"ORION'S BELT BUCKLE! OUR MOST GIFTED GIANT IS BACK!" said Madame Bogbrush. A crack like thunder roared above me. I ducked for cover.

"Don't worry," whispered Walloping. "Madame Bogbrush is happy. She's clapping her hands!"

I stood up straight again. I wasn't sure I'd ever get used to the Headteacher's many noises. They all sounded terrifying to me.

Unfortunately, she didn't stay happy for long.

"YOU..." Madame Bobgrush began.

"YOU'RE A..." I knew she was looking at me.

"YOU'RE A SMALL! IN MY SCHOOL! HOW DID THIS HAPPEN?" she roared. Her breath blew every leaf on the school field out into the swamp. I clung onto my best friend.

"Harvey saved me," said Norma.

"From Mistress Ring," said Walloping. "She's the Unchosen One!"

"HMMMM," said Madame Bogbrush, tapping her meat-pounding shoes on the wilted grass.

Ms Sugar Plum beat her wings and scribbled furiously in her clipboard. I hoped the fairy would see that we really had saved the school from grave danger.

By now, pretty much every giant had lumbered onto the field too. They stood well back from the Headteacher. Most of them pointed at me. A few of them waved bashing clubs. Others laughed at my spotty blue underpants. (I wished I hadn't lost my dancing dungarees in the sink pit.)

I stayed close to Walloping.

Madame Bogbrush stamped her feet.

"ALL I WANTED WAS TO PUT ON A BRILLIANT PERFORMANCE FOR MS SUGAR PLUM AND THE MUMS AND DADS," said Madame Bogbrush. "I WANTED TO SHOW THEM SOMETHING THEY'D NEVER SEEN BEFORE. BUT OUR GRAND FINALE SPELL IS RUINED. OUR MAGIC TEACHER'S DISAPPEARED. AND FROM WHAT I'VE SEEN TODAY, GIANTS CAN'T DANCE." She gave a heavy sigh that rushed through the field like a gale. A few of the younger giants blew into the bushes. "I CAN'T STOMP ON

ALL OF YOU ... NOT WHEN MS SUGAR PLUM'S WATCHING." (The look on the fairy's grumpy face said she might not have minded.) "WE'LL HAVE TO DO SYNCHRONISED GRUNTING IN OUR END OF TERM PERFORMANCE. JUST LIKE EVERY YEAR."

The giants hung their heads. Tears and dribble puddled on the ground.

I was confused. Madame Bogbrush was talking about the performance, not about me. Did that mean she wasn't going to stomp on me? Could I stay in school?

"GO AND REHEARSE," she said.

I turned to follow the others back to the stomping ground. I still had a chance to bring Mum and Dad back together by impressing them in the show. I hoped they liked grunting.

"NOT YOU, SMALL," said Madame Bogbrush. Her shiny red shoes slammed down in front of me.

"I'LL DECIDE WHAT TO DO WITH YOU ... AFTER THE PERFORMANCE."

And I felt like I was sinking in the swamp all over again.

Chapter twenty-five

It's Not Your Fault

For the first time in weeks, my arms didn't hurt, my stomach didn't ache, and no one asked if I needed the toilet. But all I wanted was to wobble round on my stupid stilts like nothing had happened.

I decided to go back to the Fortune Teller in the Cellar. Now every student and teacher was rehearsing on the stomping ground, visiting her would be easy.

The fortune teller probably couldn't tell me if I'd be stomped out of school. Or if I'd lose my best friend for good. Even so, I hoped she might give me some clues.

The cellar candles burned as brightly as before. And the cobwebs were just as sticky.

"I've been expecting you," said the Fortune Teller in the Cellar. She still looked like Mum, but she definitely wasn't.

I wished real Mum was here.

"No need to thank me," said the fortune teller. "You're welcome."

"What?" I spluttered. Last time I was here she wasn't exactly helpful.

The fortune teller smiled.

"You looked before you leaped, didn't you? You wouldn't be here if you hadn't."

"But why didn't you tell me Mistress Ring was the evil Ring Mistress?" I asked. "Why did you let me drink sleeping potion? And *why* didn't you tell me how to save Norma?" I struggled to keep my voice level.

She sighed, strumming her fingers on top of her crystal ball. "I couldn't. I've already told you: I know how stories start, not how they end. Which is better, don't you think? It's much more exciting to work the end out for yourself."

"So, you can't tell me if Madame Bogbrush is going to stomp me into a sandwich?" I asked.

The fortune teller looked at me sadly, then stared hard into her crystal ball.

"I see Madame Bogbrush and a great crowd of giants," she began.

"Yes," I said, leaning forward.

"Madame Bogbrush has an important message for you."

"Yes…" I said again. My stomach bubbled.

"She says…"

Thud.

The fortune teller's head slumped over her crystal ball. She started to snore.

"No!" I cried, shaking her shoulder. "Wake up! Please!"

"Huh? Oh," said the fortune teller. Her eyes sprang open.

"I'm sorry Harvey Small, it can't be done. I can't see any further than that."

I fell into the chair in front of her and sighed.

She shrugged apologetically. "I can tell you this, though," she said. "It's not your fault."

"What's not my fault?" I said.

The fortune teller stared at me.

I knew what she was trying to tell me.

"I'm not the Unchosen One?" I said. "Yeah, I kind of figured that out."

"It's not your fault," she said again, still staring at me. "Any of it."

Out of nowhere, my eyes prickled.

"Your parents didn't split up because of you," she carried on.

I so wished that was true.

My bottom lip wobbled.

"But, my old football boot. When Dad tripped over it, he..." I began.

"They split up because, no matter how much they

loved you, they wanted to throttle each other more," she said.

I blinked hard. For the first time in forever I didn't feel like I was carrying the weight of a giant's bashing club on my back.

"Oh, and you're right, you're not the Unchosen One," she added.

We all knew that.

"You're the Chosen One," she said.

I stared at her.

"W-what?" I said. There weren't any Chosen Ones in the predictions.

"I know what you're thinking. "There weren't any Chosen Ones in my predictions.""

She was good.

"By trying so hard *not* to be the Unchosen One, you saved the giants from the Unspeakable Circus. You. A Small."

Just for a moment, I felt my cheeks glow.

"Now the giants need you. You're *good* news, Harvey Small. Whatever happens next, remember that," she said.

"But what *will* happen next? Why do the giants need a Chosen One?" I asked.

"Ahaa," said the fortune teller, peering back into her crystal ball. "That's because…"

Thud.

She was asleep. Again.

Chapter twenty-six

The Show Goes On

GRRRRUNT!
    Stomp.
GRRUNT! GRRRRUNT! GRRUUUUUUNNNT!
Stomp.
Stomp.
"Ow!"
"Shhhh!"
"Wave those handkerchiefs higher, giants!"

The noise of my classmates rehearsing rumbled through the castle grounds. But it was the fortune teller's words that clanged in my ears. "You're the Chosen One," she said. When you've spent your

WHOLE LIFE being bad news, it's pretty hard to believe a prediction like that.

I bet Madame Bogbrush wouldn't believe it either. No. Tomorrow would be my last day at giant school, and I'd have to move and make friends all over again. Just like usual.

Rurrooghhh!

Hang on. I'd know that rattling trumpet anywhere. I looked around me. Twinkle the skelephant was hiding between the tall trees! She must have plodded through the gate when Madame Bogbrush was telling us all off. Luckily, Madame Bogbrush was nowhere near. Being a half-living, half-dead elephant was almost certainly against her rules.

I threw my arms round Twinkle's bony legs (without my stilts I couldn't reach any higher).

"Looks like it's just you and me now, eh girl?" I said. Would Mum let me keep her as a pet? I doubted it.

Twinkle raised a friendly shadow trunk, dropping her shiny leather football at my feet.

I couldn't resist giving it a quick keepie-uppie kick.

Then another.

And another.

Before I knew it, I was grinning like a loon. I'd hardly played any football since Dad left. But I could still do my old tricks.

I bounced the ball on my knee, then dropped it onto my toes … and back to my knee, and down to my toes.

"*Rurooooghh!*" trumpeted Twinkle, swishing her shadow tail.

"One, two, three…" I counted. Then I headed the ball to Twinkle.

The ball soared up … up … up…

And Twinkle caught it in the end of her shadow trunk and threw it right back! It turns out she's a natural footie star! No wonder she carried that ball everywhere.

"That's my girl!" I said.

For a few minutes, I forgot about the Ring Mistress, and Madame Bogbrush and being the Chosen One.

I just kept kicking and passing the ball to Twinkle. Twinkle caught it every time.

It gave me a brilliant idea.

A brilliant idea that might just impress Ms Sugar Plum enough to save the school.

*

Ms Sugar Plum flapped by me looking gleeful. "Enjoy your last day, bozo!" cried the inspector, whacking me with her clipboard as she flitted to the stomping ground. She probably thought it was going to be *everyone's* last day. Could the giant's performance ever pass the Beastly School Board Inspection?

Mums and dads had already arrived from every corner of the swamp. Their chatter carried across the courtyard.

"*Of course, my Lumbering Turnip has always been a natural at stomping, he gets it from his Pa…*"

"*Gallumphing's struggled a bit with crushing things this year, but his club swinging is so much better now.*"

I wished Mum and Dad were here, too. But they didn't know the secret I was planning.

Walloping was wearing a yellow bow tie and his best grunting socks and dungarees (they were blue with white stripes). He looked smart.

"Wishes me luck!" he said, as the bone-blasting show bells clanged.

DING!

DING!

DING!

I raced to the tall trees to get Twinkle. The skelephant could watch the show with me, hidden behind the third bell tower. The mums and dads were so busy whooping and cheering their kids on, they'd never notice Twinkle's shadowy ears flapping.

"Places everyone! Hurry now!" said Mrs Mahoosive, clapping her hands.

Toot-toot-screeech-toot!

Mr Ogg played the trumpet. Mrs Mahoosive sat next to him, shouting instructions.

"One, two, three, *stomp!*"

"One, two, three, *swing!*"

"One, two, three, *grunt!*"

The class swung their clubs and stamped their feet and grunted together – grinning the whole way through. I don't know why Madame Bogbrush wanted to change a thing. It was brilliant.

When the class finished, the parents roared with applause, kicking up thick clouds of stomping dust and making the heavy, stone bell tower shake. I clung to Twinkle's bony legs to stop myself blowing away.

My tummy felt like it was filled with somersaulting swamp moths. It was almost time for THE PLAN.

When the applause ended, Madame Bogbrush's shiny red shoes crashed down in front of the stage.

"GIFTED GIANT PARENTS, THIS YEAR I WANTED TO SHOW YOU THINGS YOU'D NEVER SEEN BEFORE. BUT IN THE END, WE DECIDED…"

Walloping thudded over to me. He stuck his thumbs in the air and clambered onto Twinkle's back.

I took a gigantic breath. This was my chance. I led Twinkle across the middle of the stomping ground, in front of Ms Sugar Plum and right in front of the mums and dads.

Ms Sugar Plum dropped her clipboard.

The parents gasped.

Some stood up.

Others clenched their fists.

"It's a … a … a…" they began.

"**Skelephant!**" they said, clapping their huge hands over their mouths.

"**And you…**" they said, glaring at me.

"**You is…**" they spluttered.

"He's a Small," said Norma Enormous, marching into the middle of the stomping ground. "And he saved me from the Unspeakable Circus!"

"Huh?" said all the mums and dads at once – scratching their heads. They looked just like my classmates.

I picked up Twinkle's circus football and kicked…

Knee.

Toe.

Head.

Twinkle.

My toes tingled. My heart pounded. I didn't stop, I just kept kicking the ball. Twinkle's grey shadow twinkled brighter with every pass.

"That's it, best friend. Catch!" said Walloping, throwing the school's smallest bashing club towards me. I caught it *at the same time* as kicking the ball back to Twinkle. (All my juggling practice finally paid off.)

"Yeah!" yelled Gallumphing, bashing his hands together.

Norma Enormous cartwheeled around me in sparkling circles (she'd pulled her glittery dancing leotard over her grunting dungarees).

I kicked and threw and caught. Twinkle trumpeted and twinkled. Walloping threw clubs and cheered. Norma tumbled and flipped – all the while telling the story of how I'd saved her. And my classmates clapped in time, surrounding me on the stomping ground.

Clap. Clap. Clap.

Kick. Kick. Kick.

For a second, I could have sworn I saw Ms Sugar Plum SMILE.

One by one, the parents sat down to watch.

"Well, I've never seen *that* before," said one.

"Me neither, what an excellent performance," said another.

"That's *our* boy," said a third.

I looked up and almost dropped my bashing club.

Mum and Dad were sitting in the third row.

Chapter twenty-seven

A True Giant

Can you believe it? Mum and Dad were actually *here*.

Together.

With all the *giant mums and dads*.

"You didn't think we'd miss your show, did you?" said Dad, when I left the stomping ground.

"But, how did you … why are you…?" I began. I looked round nervously. I hoped no one would stomp them into sandwiches.

"Madame Bogbrush told us what happened," said Mum, wobbling onto her feet.

Of course. Mum and Dad were wearing stilts!

Norma Enormous clomped over and put a sweaty

hand on my shoulder. "Madame Bogbrush told them you're a hero," she said. "Good finale, by the way. You made my cartwheeling look *even* better."

"We thought you were *brilliant*," said Mum.

"So, are you back together?" I asked Mum. My insides fluttered with hope.

"Goodness no," she said, shaking her head.

I tried not to look crushed.

"But that doesn't mean we can't put on a pair of stilts and sit in the same stomping ground as each other," said Dad.

"For a few minutes," said Mum.

"For you," they said, hugging me from both sides.

Maybe the Fortune Teller in the Cellar was right. Maybe it *wasn't* my fault they broke up. And, well, they did look … happy. Loads happier than when they lived together. Maybe things were better this way.

"We've bought you a present," said Mum. She handed me a package wrapped in crumpled red paper. Mum had an eager look in her eyes I'd seen before. So did Dad.

I opened it.

"Plastic fangs?" I said, looking at the fake pointy teeth. Why couldn't they just buy me football boots?

"We've found a new school for you, a really good one," said Dad. He pulled a long black cloak out of his bag and wrapped it round my shoulders.

My stomach twisted. For a minute I'd almost forgotten I'd have to move again.

"Viscount Bloodsucker's School for High Achieving Vampires gets *excellent* results," said Mum.

"And you can start straight after the holidays," said Dad.

"Great," I said. But I didn't think it was great. Not even a little bit.

Madame Bogbrush's meat

pounder shoes *CLICKETY CLACKETY CLACKED* down in front of Mum and Dad.

"I DON'T THINK FANGS WILL BE NECESSARY," said the Headteacher, blowing Mum and Dad back into their seats.

"Huh?" I said.

"Huh?" said a crowd of gifted giants.

"Huh?" said a crowd of all the gifted giants' mums and dads.

"HARVEY IS A SMALL. AND NORMALLY, I DON'T LIKE SMALLS."

Madame Bogbrush hovered a long, wrinkled finger above my head.

"BUT I WAS WRONG. SMALLS AREN'T ALL BAD. *THIS* SMALL HAS SAVED OUR BEST STUDENT FROM GRAVE DANGER. HE'S MADE OUR PERFORMANCE EXTRAORDINARY." She smiled at me. "YOU'RE A TRUE GIANT," said Madame Bogbrush.

I stared open-mouthed up at Madame Bogbrush. I scratched my head. I was so surprised, I think I even dribbled.

"I WOULD BE DELIGHTED TO HAVE YOU IN MY SCHOOL ... IF WE PASS OUR INSPECTION."

All eyes squinted at Ms Sugar Plum. The candyfloss-shaped fairy finally stopped scribbling on her clipboard.

The inspector tutted.

Please let us pass. Please let us pass. Please let us pass. I thought.

Then she said, "Hmm."

Would I be leaving the school after all?

Finally, she shrugged her shoulders and sighed. "Here's my report. You've passed my inspection. I suppose."

And the whole school cheered all over again.

"Yippeeeeeeeee!" said Walloping, thumping me on the back and sending me stumbling halfway across the stomping ground.

"And the skelephant?" said Jumbolina, looking up at Madame Bogbrush. "Can we keep the skelephant?"

Since the end of the show, the whole class had taken turns to ride Twinkle. They silently stared up at the Headteacher, putting on their very best pleading faces.

"**AND THE SKELEPHANT…**" said Madame Bogbrush, with a sigh. "**…CAN STAY. BUT YOU'LL HAVE TO LOOK AFTER HER, NOT ME.**"

We whooped and cheered.

Twinkle trumpeted.

My heart felt fuller than an overinflated football.

I am Harvey Small, not Harvey Tall. But today, staring up past the knobbly knees, and sausage hands and dribbly grins of my classmates, I've never felt more like a giant.

The end. Almost.

Does Madame Bogbrush's School for Gifted Giants pass the inspection?

I suppose so, yes.

Giants need more varied lessons to stretch their brains instead of their arms. I still don't know if they can spell. But their stomping, grunting and clomping is the best I've ever seen.

It's true that the future panics them. But this makes them even braver when they fight grave danger and live to tell the tale.

Recommendations:

Keep the sneaking, whispering boy with the small hands, wobbly walk, bloody nose and three-headed worm who wants to vanish, stands still in tap dancing and saved the school. He's good news.

Meanwhile, in the biggest house in Small City...

The Fortune Teller in the Cellar's twin sister, Cordelia Stinkington-Rich, sips champagne and opens her jewellery box. Gleaming jewels spill onto the dressing table.

She can't decide. Should she wear pearls to the party tonight? Or the diamonds? Or maybe the rubies? She glances into the heavy glass ball on her dressing table, looking for answers. And tonight's lottery numbers.

Clouds swirl inside the crystal ball.

Cordelia's eyes glaze over, just like always.

She hears herself speak to the empty room, just like always.

"Beware. The Unchosen One lands while the fanged ones sleep. Grave danger strikes again," she says.

Cordelia tears her eyes away from the glass ball and frowns. That wasn't the fashion advice she expected. Fangs haven't been on *any* of the catwalks.

Still, she wipes away her marshmallow pink lipstick and tries a new shade.

Yes, *blood* red is much better.

She wraps a long black cloak around her shoulders and stalks into the night, leaving her invitation on the dressing table.

It doesn't matter. Cordelia Stinkington-Rich is always invited in.

Acknowledgements

You wouldn't be reading this book if it weren't for so many people, who all deserve double helpings of hot chocolate with whipped cream, chocolate sprinkles and marshmallows. Here they are (in order of appearance):

My parents – for obvious biological reasons but more importantly for their constant love and support. Mum has always been the best and toughest beta reader out there.

Nick – for love, roast potatoes, and endless patience as I witter on about made-up worlds at every opportunity.

Neil Gaiman – whose 'Make Good Art' speech pushed me to sign up for a City Lit children's writing course.

Lou Kuenzler – for running that course and turning me into the writer I am today.

Matilde, Lisa, Jo, Nick, Cath, Beth, Varsha and anyone else in the pub that night after City Lit who said, 'yeah, that giant idea of yours sounds fun. You should write it.'

Terrie – for daily writing cheer, weekly writing sessions and teaching me how to use Twitter.

Harvey – for lending me his name (his brother and parents are pretty awesome, too).

Lydia – my wonderful agent, for believing in me and sending my stories into the world. Huge thanks to the whole Darley Anderson team, too.

Mikka – for believing in Small! enough to buy it and publish it in this beautiful book.

Rory – illustrator extraordinaire, for turning my ramblings into mind-bogglingly good illustrations.

Holly – for turning those illustrations into a cracking cover.

2022 Debuts and the Forever Unannounced Twitter groups – for sharing the journey with me.

For every early reader and supporter for saying nice things and helping Small! find its way.

You – for reading Small! all the way to the end. Thank you.